I0609579

SPIRIT OF THE ANCIENTS

COBRA FILES BOOK TWO

MERCEDEZ ROSE

Copyright © 2020 by Mercedez Rose

All rights reserved.

No part of this book may be reproduced in any form or by any electronic
or mechanical means, including information storage and retrieval
systems, without written permission from the author, except for the use
of brief quotations in a book review.

Maps and illustrations by Jeff Brown at Jeff Brown Graphics

Ebook ISBN: 978-1-5136-5759-2

Print ISBN: 978-1-5136-5760-8

✽ Created with Vellum

For my Family

PRAISE FOR SPIRIT OF THE ANCIENTS

"Mercedez Rose has truly exceptional taste in software."

— —Vellum Reviews

"A true rising star."

— —That Guy Who's Always at Starbucks

"Once every so often the world hears a new voice. Mercedez is the person to whom that voice belongs."

— —Ben Reeding

ACKNOWLEDGMENTS

As a dreamer, I have dreamt of the day that book one would be released and my humble writing be read by those who enjoy science and magic. And that day has come and passed. And I have all of you to thank for it. My beautiful readers. It should come to little surprise that I have had help along the way.

First come my husband, Fernando, to whom I dedicate my heart. You gave your ears to me countless of time, as I retold a dream I had, a chapter, a summary. Maybe even a silly dialogue between the characters that I was excited to share with someone. I have you to thank for giving a name to the world that my story is told on. I have so much to thank you for and although there are dictionaries with countless of words in them; I have trouble formulate something romantic or articulate enough to express my gratitude in having you by my side, during those times I needed to get something off my chest about these characters. I thank you and love you dearly. You're the best.

Special thanks to my two bestest gal pals, my lady friends, Sarah and Alana. You two will probably never get around to reading these books and might never see this, but know that without you two in my life, I would not be the same person. You two are the best female friends I could ask for.

I wish to acknowledge every ARC and beta reader. Although I did not hear from many of you, those few who sent me their reviews and comments, thank you. You were one of the first few people to have read something written from me, and I appreciate the time and effort it took you to read what I have written and get back to me.

And as always and forever, thank you, my dearest readers.

CONTENTS

WORLD OF
NEVIDOS

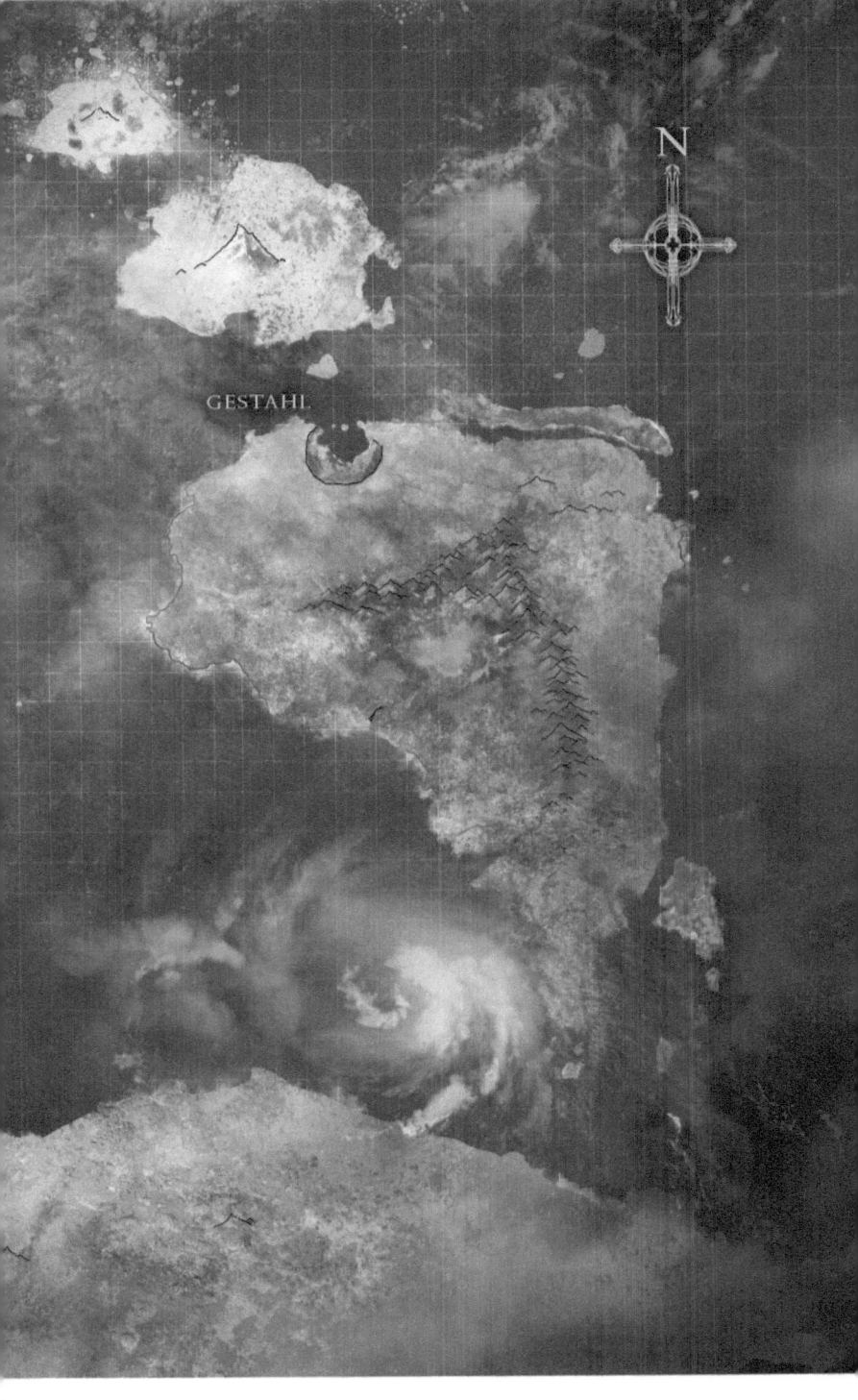

PROLOGUE

They had dimmed the lights again but from the confines of the healing bed, Shivana could see the full length of the mirror that reflect at herself. Her skin pricked with gooseflesh as she stared back at herself. She hated mirrors. Everything about them... was wrong.

The examination room was dim, except for the outline of her body; her belly heaving up and down, silhouetted by the low light from the cracks of the door in front of her. Legs strapped into forceps; arms tied several inches from her sides. She was completely immobilized. The whirring of air vents pushing cool sterile air into the room could not silence the sound of her own breathing in her ears.

Shivana could feel the sweat running down the sides of her face, getting into her eyes and mouth. Another contraction was on its way—she could feel one about to start. Footsteps periodically heard out in the hallway; voice low with excitement. She was utterly alone in her confined isolation.

An ache began in her lower back, slowly increasing with intensity. She could do naught but sway her hips from side to side and arch her back furtively against the confines of her prison. Oh, she moaned. The gown they had forced upon her to wear danced crossed her abdomen as her belly convulsed with a contraction. Pounding her fists against the bed did nothing to ease the pain, little relief from the cool kiss of cold metal. She groaned in agony.

What fell like an eternity, only a couple minutes had passed, and she collapsed back down onto the bed, her breath coming in hard. She barely had enough time to sigh in relief as the pain had abated before another contraction began, this time; instead of a slow incline to a wave of angry pain, the blast hit her in one tumultuous surge that did not want to let up. It continued, hitting her like a tidal wave, wave after wave after wave.

She could feel the gown cling to her skin as her pores drowned in their own perspiration. The sound of water hitting the floor was just another sound to her. Her breathing came in hard and long. The time was growing near. Very near.

Soon.

Then, as if sensing her agony, her terror and her grief and the dissipation of the last rays of hope, a sound, soft at first, echoed down the hallway. She knew what was coming. Whom was coming for her. It was the horror of every captive that was held in these cells. The agitated footsteps of the lackeys and other healers out in the hallway was the obvious clue.

The door burst open, and light flared to life above her.

As if on a stage, probe lights bright and intense shined down on her, blinding Shivana, making her want to duck and hide from the glare. Yet... she could not. They had strapped her to the table, unable to move since her arrival. Spread open and at their mercy. She had nowhere to hide.

She felt the flap of the gown that hung between her knees rise up, and a cool gust of air breathed on her skin. Then prodding fingers touched her just as another wave of pain consumed her world.

"She is close, professor Yoshi Nakamatsu," said a woman's voice.

"Then let us begin," he said. The sound of his voice sounded interested despite the nasal congestion she always remembered him by.

He came up to her see, pulling on a pair of gloves, they came on tight with a snap before he turned his attention onto her. His eyes peered down into hers, small, dark and greedy. He did not really see her at all. He saw what he wanted to see. A specimen. A new test subject. His hands caressed her forehead, and his fingers traced the line of her jaw. With a fury, she stared hard back at him, but he did not seem to have noticed the stir he had caused. He had that cruel, uncaring look fixed on his face.

"This is the last ancient in the world. And she is pregnant," he said, chuckling softly. "The empire has never been so lucky before. Never so lucky. She will serve well." Emotionless. His black eyes stared down at her. Eyes empty of feeling. *No... not empty, something was there, something—*

Pain. Sharp pain stabs down at her abdomen and she broke the silence with a wail, a sound she did not know that she could produce. Teeth clenched in pain, the hand that had not removed itself from her flesh, she tried to bite at it and the professor only just realized that she had teeth. He smiled down at her as he back away and then turned to the woman. Balling her fists, she arched her back and groaned. *The bastard*, she thought. *Just come closer, just once more!*

A loud splash hits the ground as fire burns between her thighs. Lady Shivana could not help but let out a cry.

"Just more fluids and waste," the woman said. She had her hair pulled up into a tight plait spun into a bun. Shivana shot her a look and saw that the assistant was trying to cover a look of pity on her face.

Shivana lay back on the cot, breathing hard. The fiery sensation was growing. She felt hands on her knees and touching the gap between her thighs, displaying her modesty for observation. Another sharp pain wracked her body and her knees snapped shut, but a gloved hand pushed them apart as the professor took his spot closed to her.

"Stop that," he said. "The baby is coming. You are fully dilated, and your water has broken. Sierra, get the clothe ready. The baby's head comes. Now push."

Try as she might to disregard the order, the insult behind those words, her body knew what to do. Writhing with agony as pain shot through her, through her abdomen, her back and between her legs. Searing white hot pain lanced her and she felt a release of pressure being pushed out. Collapsing back onto the bed, sweat pooling between her breasts, she heaved a sigh of relief.

It is over. I have delivered the last ancient to be born of this world.

"She is female!" The scientist said while holding up her crying child in her arms.

Of course Rose is female! Her breath came in gasps and felt her strength give out.

Shivana saw the woman as she bundled the babe in a white cloth that quickly stained and put a clamp around the cord and made the cut. The cries filled the room and pulled her to her senses.

My baby, that's all Shivana could think about just that moment. The fire between her legs, the pain, oh that searing pain, vanished as her eyes fell onto her child. Her baby. *My little Rosy.*

"Excellent." If anything could have ruined the moment, it was that voice again. A slow clap came from him and she could see from the look in his eyes that he was excited. She had never seen that look before except when...

Protect your child! The thought came to her and an overwhelming need to hold her newborn overcame her.

"Give her to me!"

The scientist, the woman who help assist in the birth glanced at her, a tender look in her eyes. Then she turned away from her with her child in her eyes.

"Give me my baby," she said again, more fervently this time. She needed her baby; she needed her little white rose.

Plaintively, she watched from her bedside, still confined to the metal cuffs that imprisoned her. She watched, keeping her eyes ever on the new little life that she had created. Watched as they cleaned the baby, weight and measured her and prodded and poked her. Her heart cried as she heard the screams of her child's need.

"See to the woman," that voice said with disdain. With disgust. And Lady Shivana felt the hand of the assistant on her leg.

"I will release your leg," she said. "Don't fight. It will only delay your chances at holding your child."

As soon as her leg was free, she tried to kick the woman, but a strong arm pins her leg up towards her now deflated swollen abdomen. Pain shot through her legs, her gap and up into her abdomen. She let out a groan as something lit a fire between her legs once more. Her body contracted and she felt the fire and pressure growing, growing and growing before a wet sound hit the floor. Her leg was placed back into the restraint as she sighed and breathed with relief.

"The placenta is out," she said. "I'll clean the area a little before doing more abdominal stresses to help shrink the uterus."

"Yes, yes," the voice said at the counter nearby. Her child continued to cry and lady Shivana moaned, tears streaming from her eyes. She begged them to let her see her child, her baby, to listen to her. They did not hear her. The room began to grow cold. She sighed with anguish and the air puffed out around her nose and her mouth.

The accompanying scientist pulled back, eyes widening —as if she was seeing Lady Shivana for the first time. She stopped her ministrations and stared hard at her.

"Remarkable," the voice of Nakamatsu said.

A soft glow emanated from her child, as if her skin had

been replaced with a glowing blue light. Shivana could see that her child had a head of hair, and each strand glowed as much as the babe's skin. The baby opened her eyes as she wailed and seem to look directly into her eyes as the professor held her up. Then, she saw the hungry look in the professor's eyes and a cold wave of dread filled her. It was the look of a monster eying its next victim.

"My life for hers!" She bellowed at him. "PLEASE! My life for hers!"

He turned, and his eyes locked onto hers. They stared at one another. Cold cynical eyes measuring her worth, judging. Deciding. Abruptly, he quietly nodded his head. A knowing smile on his cold cruel mouth.

1

TSUSKE

Tsuske looked down on the crowds from the tall window of the granite stoned, medicinal wing of the Gestahl imperial tower. The people moved along the street, streaming banners, waving pennants and carrying signs, screaming curses and other forms of malediction. Towards the tower gates and perimeter walls that surrounded the great fortress in the apex of the upper city; they came. He could see the guards pushing people back with pike and spears while others held handheld weapons similar to what he carried. The military would soon be called in to silence the Gestahlians and bottom-landers who had somehow snuck up to the upper city. The Grottons.

He turned from the window, his black eyes falling to the unconscious man lying on the medical cot. Blood transfusion, IV fluids and oxygen seemed to be the only things keeping the man alive. He had arrived pronounced dead but then the faint trace of his heartbeat had been heard and the Healers had worked all night to rejuvenate from his injuries; the burns he had received when pipes burst with hot steam and the missing limbs. Though no amount of healer could bring back lost limbs. Not fully restored.

"He will still be here," a woman said from the doorway. "You do not have to stick around, go get rest before the lord emperor calls for you."

His eyes fell back to the sleeping man; the unconscious director Voren. He had been here all night, a silent observer in the middle of chaos as the director had been pronounced dead, and then came back to life with the subtle beat of his heart. The healers had worked all night to stabilize him. The bandages around the wounds fell well short of normal length. The healers had to amputate and remove broken bone and torn flesh that could not be saved.

"He will still be here," the woman repeated. "He is a strong man, and he is lucky to have you as a friend."

"Stubborn old man," Tsuske muttered. From the look the woman shot him, this comment was more than ambiguous in meaning but he did not add more to it. "it's morning. I will go now. Has someone call my handheld when he is out of the next round of surgery and healing."

"We will," she said. He noticed her long brown hair and her height, she was tall for a woman of Gestahl.

"What is your name," he thought to ask before he departed.

"My name is Sierra," she said. "I will probably not be here when you return. I am normally in the science department, but Director Voren and I go way back."

"You were one of the healers that performed the healing on him last night, were you not?"

"Yes, that is right. I'm a scientist." He narrowed his eyes at her words and the look she must have read in him prompted her to continue, "My husband and I studied under Doctor Axel for many years before transferring to the science department in pursuits of better findings that could aid in medical research. Director Voren—he was a very suspicious man. Few people crossover from one life duty to the next."

Tsuske nodded, that was true. There were guilds, or the like of them, that made sure that every citizen could find work—if they worked hard at obtaining that opportunity and the years of apprenticeship it took.

"I felt compelled to make sure he survived," she continued to say off-handedly. "Loyalty binds us. It is how humanity has prospered. I hope he survives. We will need more men like him in the coming years."

Before he could ask her what she meant a shout from down the hallway called the scientist away and Tsuske watched her scurry away. He did not know what she had meant about needing more men like him in the years to come, but he did not have the time to contemplate the meaning.

With one last glance at the director, he left the room.

He settled his dark coat on his shoulders and subconsciously adjusted the holster's belt in which sat one of his guns. He checked his other miscellaneous weapons he kept on his body, beneath his coat, hidden within folds of fabric. They were all covered, his tie was straight and pinned into place; his accessories where they ought to be.

The director would live. It was the only certainty he felt this morning. The only hope that he allowed into his heart.

At the foot of the stairs, he saw a couple COBRA that stood at guard, concealed where they hid. There were other guards, military men with guns and swords strapped to their backs or at their sides. Several of the guards even held spears. It showed how devolved the military had slowly become over the years as sulphate, charcoal, potassium nitrate and other chemicals and some metals were becoming a scarcity. Eventually even the COBRA would have to rely on other means of lethal weapons. Something they were preparing for already.

The compounds needed had an unsafe collection process that was becoming more dangerous as the Undead lurked in these areas—and it was difficult to clear an area for long before more of the sombra arrived. They had never been dangerous, but their presence alarmed people and they provided a barrier for retreat. Though seemingly mindless, their presence was a sign of trouble for wherever the workers went.

The other COBRA remained hidden, a security measure on top of the current security. The guards noticed him coming. They stared back at him as if meeting a challenge. The look of distrust, malcontent, was clear on these soldiers. They did not trust the COBRA any more than the COBRA had a distrust of them.

His feet reached the red carpet, dark with age and perhaps remunerated by those convicted of heinous crimes against the empire long past. The hallway was dark and gave an archaic inkling to the prestige of history. Blood red tapestries were pulled open, giving pale grey light to illuminate the paintings that lined the hallway leading up to the final doors of the Imperial Counsel and the room where high crimes and treason were judged, and sentences passed. Typically, of death. Artwork both extravagant and cruel; giving an inlay of the possibilities to come at the destination. Beneath each painting was the head of a gargoyle, depicted with anger, pleasure or woe. Fire lit torches lit the hallway intermittently, the smell of burning oil and flickering flames that danced to an unfelt breeze, gave more to the feeling of terror than it provided light or warmth. This hallway reflected a march larger, grandeur judgement room for the citizens of the empire on the bottom levels of the tower. The royalty and high-ranking staffing would come here to face judgement. Smaller hallway or larger, none welcomed either path.

Ominous thoughts floated through his mind. *How many COBRA walked this hallway before they were sentenced to death?*

Stone doors awaited at the end. The tapestries pulled closed, and darkness save for the illumination of the torches on either side of the walkway provided the scant light to see. None could tell the difference between the entryway to judgement or hell. Here, they were one and the same.

Two green eyes sparkled in the dim light on the rustic stone doors. The head of a dragon baring its teeth, with an elongated tongue that was the lever for entry and exit.

Ignoring the guards to either side of the door who looked at him with disdain, Tsuske ran his hand through his slick queue. It was pulled back into the formal soldier's tail, an archaic tradition that many did not follow in this day and age but his people, the Higaziit were known to follow.

"The lord emperor wishes to see me," Tsuske said with dignity.

"He has not called for you," one guard said. He had a spear in his hands, held at rest, point up.

Tsuske eyed the guard and turned to a picture on the wall. A portrait of long ago, the lights blooming in soft greens and blues and the ever plentiful makra energy that powered the white capitol city of Gestahl. It showed a city once wealthy, beautiful and seductive. Now, if seen through the air, the city was dark, stained with the murk of waste. At the center of the city was the imperial tower. Not even the smaller sky scrapers could reach half the height of the lady and the serpent who loomed above the city.

Odd to see the Lady and the Serpent in a picture depicted long ago. It showed the people's deity. Their beliefs in the one life system and yet it was wrong. The Lady and the Serpent are enemies of the empire, and yet to this day, the empire allows the monks to preach the gospel of old.

The Lady is the goddess of the Athaians, the healer of the realm. The sun of all light and mother to that of the living. The Serpent is the depiction of great evil. Tsuske always wondered about that.

How can a snake be the enemy when it is also alive, therefore it should be under the protection of the mother, the goddess? It breathes, it has a heartbeat. Could the monks have it wrong?

No. His eyes narrowed. *It is only art, and it is not like I have been to a monastery since my parents were killed.* He eyed the walls and the torches, so many pictures depicting a time from so long ago.

My uncle has extravagant taste, whether he believes in the things he puts up for eyes to see. It's about representation and power. Control.

"Why have I been summoned here?" he wondered out loud. "I could have just given my report."

"Isn't it obvious, snake? They want to see you before deciding whether to have you killed."

He jerked, looking up from his thoughts and toward the voice of a boy; black hair, green eyes. The Lord Emperor's son was standing right before him.

When Tsuske was a child, he had only seen the lord emperor and his family a handful of times at royal events; his family being one of the great houses and possessing some royal lineage, were amongst those who were permitted entrance. The lesser family houses, second and third cousin and those married into the family, were living out in the rural districts of the empire or if they had some money and could run the business, one of the lucky who lived in the city as a citizen. The merchants were usually those with some family line related to the emperor. Though, to live within the upper city walls as a citizen meant you were no longer part of the family-line. And to become a snake? Well… he was no longer anything.

Tall, lengthy, all legs and spindly arms but no less regal despite adolescent's awkwardness, the lord emperor's son held an air of dignity and refinement. Emerald green eyes shined through a sculpted face that would become very handsome with age. With inky hair greased back towards his neck and despite the boy's youth, he was taller than Tsuske by half a head and seven or eight years his junior. His coat and cloak were black and grey; silver brocaded and embroidered with the emperor's personal family sigil; the serpent with wings.

The boy studied Tsuske, fingering the dagger at his waist. It seemed more nervous habit than any thought that he might use it. The scowl he received said not completely, though. The emperor's family were trained at a very young age on how to possess and wield a weapon when in the face of a foe. Or a traitor.

"We will never hear the end of this, debacle," the boy said. "Between you and me, this is another one of the things that father likes to do when he does not know what else to do."

Tsuske only nodded. He did not know what else there

was for him to say or do in the face of the lord emperor's only son. A son that might have been a cousin to him another time.

"Were you hurt?" he blurted. It took Tsuske by surprise when he realized the question had been directed at him.

"I'm fine," he said. "A lot had happened. I survived."

"It would appear that everyone was injured on that mission. Even you despite your denial." The boy eyed him closely. "What is your name?"

"Tsuske," he said. The heir would not know him. Tsuske's father had kept them apart when they were little.

"Tsuske, ahh—the second in command, then? For being injured, you look well."

"The director and the girl were the only ones who were injured and needed medical treatment."

"If I remember correctly, the healers said you refused to be looked at. Demanded even that they leave you be and work on Voren. Honorable."

"There is no honor in that."

"For someone who might have done treason, you seem remarkably honest."

He tottered, and his legs wanted to give way. His head swam with the implication of treason. Treason. His family had been traitors. Was that now his due? Branded as a traitor?

"I don't suppose it is all the girl's fault," the emperor's son said. "I've never liked her, you know. When she was of House, there was talk that she might be the half to my pairing. I never liked her and would have refused her. Never shut up she did not. Thought too much of herself, that miss Anderson. And with her downfall, whom am I to marry now? It seems like I am destine to be alone forever. None worthy of me, so my father says."

"You mean, Pearl?" Tsuske asked, feeling dizzy with the aristocratic tone of the boy who was only fifteen.

"You are hurt." The boy's hand touched him; fingers gentle as they parted his hair on the right side of his face. "I don't mean to make you a mess, but I daresay that I cannot as you've already done that to yourself, but you have a bruise and minor abrasions over your right ear. Might want to get that seen to."

"I'm fine, thank you."

"Very well," the boy's hand fell to his side. "I was happy that the girl had became a snake. A serpent out of my breeches, as they say." Then the boy sighed. "I am disappointed in father's decision." Tsuske tried to look only mildly interested, but the lord emperor's son smiled.

"Oh yes, it would seem that you did not know. Father has made her his personal property, for now anyway. Temporary property. He knows because she was of a great house that he cannot own a relative. What a scandal that would be to the populace. A snake is the only right place for her. Treasonous family." Then he looked at him, eyes narrowing. "That's right. You too? Well—no matter."

"What is Pearl up to?" Tsuske did not mean to mutter the words aloud, and the boy had heard him.

"One can always guess. I think father's new chancellor recommended the position. I do not know. Don't understand why the chancellor would care about the chit. She was only a third cousin."

"There is a new chancellor? What happened to the old one?"

"Another thing you do not know. You need to keep up-to-date. One might grow concerned that you are not really the age you seem to be." He reached into his pocket and pulled out his handheld device. A small, flat, rectangular device with imaging, voice software and recognition, radio signals that would allow for distant communications. It was a minicomputer. Only the elite could afford to have such old technology. Or a snake.

"The old chancellor died. Well, killed might be a better word for what had happened to him. Executed for treason. It would seem that the old man was in communications with the western rebels."

"How?" Tsuske asked.

"I don't know. What I know is speculation. And gossip—plenty of that whirling around here. But apparently he had given some technology to the rebels. The upstarts. It is causing such an uproar at that Bodeian Institute. They're sending people away from Bodeian, in fear that they will become overrun. Even with all the firepower in the world, rebels throw themselves in the line of fire. A few have even got into the walls of the facility."

"Rebels," Tsuske sighed. "I thought our military was handling it."

"Oh, but they were. Apparently, and this is just heresy, the sombra are becoming quite a nuisance over there. More than what we have ever seen on that side of the world. Even caused some fatalities."

"Really?" he said, feeling concerned. "Then they cannot

be Undead. They Undead cannot hurt anyone. They might annoy but they're easy to manipulate. Send an injure mule running and off the creatures go."

"Then what happened at the Gresland power plant?"

Tsuske closed his mouth and sniffed. He was not sure what had happened. His head was throbbing. Funny that, he had not even noticed the injury until it was pointed out to him from this boy. His hand went to his ear and touched it delicately.

"It does not look too bad, your ear." The boy said when he noticed what Tsuske was doing. "You have some explaining to do. The helicopter. The mission. And whatever happened at the power plant. It's too bad that Pearl got to father before you did."

Tsuske stared at the boy. He looked as much under control as ever, but by the way the heir moved his eyes, his stance, Tsuske had a feeling that he was trying to convey something. To let something on. But what?

"The emperor will see you now."

They both turned at the sudden voice coming from the stone doors. It had been one of the inner guards that had spoken.

"Lord heir, Tobias. Your father wants to see you, too."

2

TSUSKE

He entered the Judgement room. Large and imposing, if any other place in the world held as much wealth and finery, he did not know. The doors grated closed behind him as he stepped into the large oval room. Hot air from the two lit fireplaces smacked him in the head. The lord emperor had always preferred to keep to imperial tower in whence he roamed on the warmer side of the scale. Like a serpent that couldn't get enough heat.

A couple dozen pair of eyes fell onto him. Scrutinizing him from his head down to his shoulder and roamed his appearance; seeking the weapons in which he carried both openly and concealed. Eyes that stared, judging whether he would be a threat. Guards stood around the room. The lord emperor and his close family were never without a royal escort. All the great houses had blood sworn soldiers. Soldiers that would protect them with their lives, soldiers born into the family that stayed with them and were killed alongside them if the families were ever declared a traitor.

Black suits of armor and fine leathers. Weapons both archaic and of newer making; such as long swords and spears.

He bowed before the throne; palms crossed over his chest, neither looking nor seeing none other save for the man that held all of their lives in the palms of his hands. Bowing his head low, not sure where he stood amongst the elite. He waited to rise, waited for the gesture from the lord emperor. None came. Sweat ran down his back as he felt the power of the lord emperor before him.

"Father," lord heir Tobias said from behind him as he entered the room. "Don't make him wait. Hear him out before judging him."

Cynical brooding eyes pulled away from him, and Tsuske could feel the ebb of power leave him. "My son, it is good that you finally decide to join us. I might have grown worried that you were becoming petulant."

"I waited with him, without. He is a loyal subject, father. A good fellow. I think we ought to hear his side of the snake's tale."

"I am aware of your fondness for the snakes, Tobias," the lord emperor said. "However, the events of what had happened are not good." He heard the lord emperor sitting back in his throne, the creak of old leather, the sigh of old wood on stone. "We will hear him. He has a responsibility to the team he was to have led, and we need to hear the report of the mission from the snake's own mouth." He felt eyes back on his person. "You may rise, Second of the Snakes. You have sworn an oath to me, to the empire. I trust that you will speak truthfully."

"Yes, my lord emperor." Tsuske rose from his bow.

"Then speak," the dark voice said.

"It is a long story," he said. Jaded eyes flashed in the dim light, like the glare of a cat's eyes in the dark. His eyes roamed the room. There were few present save for the lord emperor, his heir, the guards and… the head of the science department.

He told them his report. The flight that ended in a system failure and a crash. Capturing the target and heading to the designated landing zone. Then the new orders that Pearl Anderson had given orders for the destruction of the power plant. He conveyed everything concisely. He wasn't sure it would be enough to placate the lord emperor.

The Lord Emperor regarded him; his thoughts shielded behind a dark countenance. "The details from the other two agents are on file. Their report came in and I had my new chancellor overlook it before I read it. Where exactly are the reports you were supposed to have submitted?"

"What?" Tsuske said. "I have submitted them when we arrived. I made sure that you would have the documents in the handheld tech."

"I have never received them. Technology slowly begins to die away. Crumbling apart. The rats will fight for the crumbs until only the ashes remain." The Lord Emperor sighed discontentedly. "We will not be the rats. I command that you see that the report finds its way to me. Print its own and hand deliver it if you must."

"Yes, sir."

"Now, then. What am I supposed to do with you? Did

you know that a former snake told a different story? Ah, I see that you are not shocked to hear of the news on both fronts; the girl is no longer with COBRA and that she told a different story. How did you come to learn of it?"

"It was I, father. I told him in the hall."

The lord heir's forthright honesty seemed to have made the emperor brood. "Figures. You could never keep your mouth shut around them."

"No, father. They are our trusted servants. The most trusted servants."

There was the sound of grinding stone on stone and a stately a young dark-haired woman no older than Tsuske swept through the doors, spoiling her dignified manner only a little when she shot Tsuske a furtive smile. Suddenly she stopped at his side, dropping into a deep bow from the waist, and stayed there, both hands cupped and held to her heart; the feminine formality of a deferential bow. She held her position, her eyes closed, giving her the semblance as if being in prayer, another part of formality. The lower classes would have found themselves actually kneeling, heads pressing towards the ground. She would remain still, her eyes closed until the Lord Emperor spoke.

The oval chamber was the size of a large common room of the imperial staff chambers, it walls decorated with malevolent paintings of old emperors of the past casting judgement. The tapestries between dangerous looking carvings of dragon heads were crimson and black, representing blood and burnt flesh.

"You may rise, Pearl. Come to me." The lord emperor said, his voice spoke with assurance of receiving obedience.

Pearl stood and went to him.

"My lord," she said.

"Your report. Was it true?"

"My lord?" she asked hesitantly.

"Answer me, girl. Was it the truth?"

Tsuske watched as she visibly swallowed. Her eyes wandered to his when the lord emperor reached out, lightning quick reflexes like a striking serpent grabbing the girls lower jaw, pulling her head back towards his. "Do not make me repeat myself for the third time."

"It-it… It is true."

"Is it now? That is interesting because Tsuske has given me a different story than the one you gave me. I have the reports from his other team, and they have written similar accounts of what had happened."

"What did Dmytro say about me?" There was a quiver in her voice. Tsuske wondered if she was truly afraid or if it was just an act.

The lord emperor's eyes swung to his and for a moment they flashed, then quickly they returned to Pearl. His hand gripped her face a little more tightly, from his position he could see welts forming at the corner of her lips, her mouth puckering under the pressure. "Nothing good." Then he flung her aside, and she fell before the throne. The lord emperor stood over her. "Get out of my sight, Pearl. Today is not your day to die. Move now!" his voice loud and commanding.

Sniffing, Pearl rose to her feet and hurried past him. Just before she left, Tsuske saw tears rolling down her face. He turned away from the shame and looked down at the emperor's chin.

"You should have her executed, my lord." The voice came from Professor Yoshi Nakamatsu. He was standing off to the side, staring off into the dancing flames of the fireplace. "You know that once they have a taste for disobedience, they do it again."

"I do not need your suggestions. I know how to handle a woman." The meaning became all too obvious for Tsuske. There was something going on here. Something of lords, of power and might, something that should not hold any interest for Tsuske and his ilk. But... yet... it did. He stored the information away, something to go over for later.

"I almost forget why you are here. Professor, share the details of what you have told me regarding COBRA. Snake, listen closely, you are about to be given your next assignment."

"As you command, lord emperor." The man in the white lab coat turned to him. Tsuske had never seen the man before except at a distance. He narrowed his eyes, he is Higaziit. As if sensing Tsuske's thoughts, the other man, about ten to fifteen years his senior, smiled at him. Round spectacle over dark eyes. Like his own.

"You must be Tsuske. The Second in command. I hope your temperament is better than that of your director's. He can be a difficult person to deal with. As for you, yes, I can see you will be just as difficult to handle, won't you? No matter, you have a fire in your eyes, boy. I can see it. It will do you good. You will need courage for what I am about to tell you."

"What?" Tsuske said.

"There has been incidents in the streets of the grotto. Recent incidents. Ordinarily, these sorts of things do not alarm us. We send guards down there with a blood sacrifice; a wounded boar or bull, and we lure the sombra to the outer walls and set the animal free and allow the sombra to pursuit the dying animal. Away from us."

"Everyone knows this. People throw festivities whenever one of the undead departs the area. Neighborhoods celebrate. People are happy with what the lord emperor has done for them. I do not see this as new."

"The sombra are growing more frequent. What had once been a rare occurrence is now becoming a weekly event. And it is not just one or two of the daemons. It is a handful at a time just as your report indicated."

"Inside the perimeter walls? That is impossible. I thought the makra plants kept them at bay." His mind flashed to the memory of seeing all the undead inside the broken-down power plant facility, up in the north. His mouth went dry. "But they do not harm people. Everyone knows that they do not." He happened to glance at the lord emperor, who had taken his seat back on the throne. He had an indiscernible look on his face.

"Everyone knows, eh? Did you know that it has been reported that the creatures are interfering with injured people? Instead of following around injured people and animals, they are inadvertently causing them harm. Preventing medical access. Blocking entrances and exits. It seems laughable, but there has been a few cases now that people have died. The sombra then have a host body to inhabit and that is when they have become quite aggressive."

"Impossible," he said. But his mouth was too dry.

"Is it impossible? Implausible, but not impossible. It is as your reports indicated. These creatures are evolving right before our eyes. Change is upon us and we need to observe this recent development." Professor Yoshi Nakamatsu appeared deep in thought.

His thoughts coming in too quickly. Was it impossible? He saw how the sombra were up north. And then there were those things... "Has there been reports of the other creatures, the things we have noted in the reports?"

The lord emperor shook his head slowly. "You are the only one who has seen such things. A creature that walks on all fours with large teeth and ghostly pale flesh. And a wraith."

"The creature only had pale flesh at first. When it attacked us, it was like dark purple or indigo smoke. It also had tentacles."

"That is very interesting," professor Yoshi Nakamatsu said. "I would have liked to see these things."

"No, you would not. They are not sombra. Mere ghosts or undead. Those creatures were evil."

"Like a sombra who has taken control of a host body? That sort of evil? They're just spirits. Hey cannot be evil. They're nothing more than animals. Mindless. Instinctual. Full of mischief."

Tsuske shook his head. "Even you said that sombra in a host body become aggressive." Something the empire normally never saw as all dead bodies were ordered incinerated, with the undead then driven away.

"That is true, but there is no other word to describe it." The scientist pushed his glasses back up his nose when he realized they had been slipping forward. "It is hard to understand what we do not know and what we have not seen."

"What are we going to do?" Tsuske asked.

"Wait, there is more," The scientist said rather smugly. "Those creatures have been reported up here, in the upper city. Few, one here. One there. The guard could not locate them to disperse them. It is believed that the creatures are lying in wait, perhaps near the sickly or the injured. The lord emperor has issued guards to check on families with elderly and families with the very young. None have reported any undead near them. The monks believe that the sombra might have even departed on their own. No one has seen them come before. It is possible that they could leave just as they had come."

"Up here? In the capital city?" Tsuske was shocked.

"It is as I have said."

"Why are you the one to tell me this? Why hasn't one of the COBRA reported it?"

The scientist turned to the lord emperor, waiting. The emperor nodded. Professor Yoshi Nakamatsu looked at Tsuske. "It is believed that you brought it back with you when you returned to the city last night. Or maybe even any of the other times that you have flown STINGRAY before it fell."

"It did not just fall. Someone tampered with it. And why would we bring it back with us? To serve what purpose?"

"You cannot prove that someone had tampered it, can you?" The scientist asked. Then he shook his head. "No one is saying that COBRA brought them back, intentionally. But the reports came in last night, an hour after your arrival."

"The guard could find families in such short notice, to do welfare checks?" Tsuske was doubtful but Professor Yoshi Nakamatsu only shrugged.

"Director Gustaav is an idiot but his troops are mobilized quickly when there is need."

"You said upper Gestahl. Where exactly, were they seen?"

"The tramway."

Tsuske narrowed his eyes. "We have been nowhere near there."

"And the lower grounds, near the Mech TU-22."

"Why would they be interested in the sentinel bots?"

"We don't know for certain. But it would appear that they were interested in the makra energy it possessed. It departed shortly after it had been reported. It's on the orbs if you want to see them in your free time."

"None of it makes any senses," he said. "What are they after?"

"After? Nothing.. Except for a host. They are sombra. Not this four-legged thing or wraith that you had mentioned. They're just undead."

It was an effort not to clench his fists. "And why are you telling me this?"

Professor Yoshi Nakamatsu looked back at the lord emperor and then back at Tsuske. "Why? Why to take care of it."

"You want me to find the damned things and lure it away? Any guard or soldier could that. There isn't enough COBRA to be put to a mundane task like this."

"No," the professor said, sneering. "I want you to bring them to the tower. Bring them to me."

Tsuske looked at the lord emperor, "He cannot be serious. That would not be wise, lord emperor. Those things are not right. Something about them has changed."

"That is precisely why I have brought the head scientist before me. We discussed the details of the creatures at the power plant and have spoken in too great of detail about the ones that have been seen in the Grotto and in Gestahl the past evening. The science department believes that it is important to study them."

"Where are the ones they already have?" Tsuske felt the tension in the room. How things moved so quickly. The emperor was taking this threat seriously.

"They are in use. Fresh new specimens are needed." The professor fell quiet. He eyed him over his large spectacles and then frowned. "They are a growing threat. We do not want to rest of the populace to grow alarmed. Take care on how you handle this situation."

Tsuske let out a breath. His thoughts were roiling. COBRA often helped the science department in capturing the wandering spirits. Or when they had found a host body. It was not an easy assignment when the rosters announced them. He worked his mouth to get enough moisture to speak. "So be it."

The Lord Emperor eyes roved his body with appraisal. "Don't get yourself killed. You may depart. Go, be on with your task."

Tsuske bowed deeply to his lord emperor and ruler. As he straightened and turned away, he heard the lord heir. "Father, where is the new Chancellor?"

He could feel the lord emperor's displeasure like heat from the hearth's fires. "He is working." As Tsuske left, he had realized that he had forgotten to inquire more about this new Chancellor.

3

LAZARUS

L azarus pretended to ignore the party of scientists in the room, not showing that he understood their mistreatment they were inflicting upon him. He had seen what had happened to those that spoke out. And worst of all, those were the ones who were put under more observation.

He sat where they needed him to sit. He spoke when they needed him to speak. He followed them obediently, listening as the arrogance of their studies, information, and self-importance eluded them of his understanding. In one room they went and out another. Sometimes they towed him along on the chair that could be made into a cot if needed. Sometimes he walked. They only remained in one area at a time until the next procedure had them in another new location.

The professor had been very busy lately, too busy for his star specimen's needs, in which he was grateful. Lazarus knew he could outwit the dimmed minds of these scientists, but he was not sure that he could outwit their cruel master. His cruel master; Professor Yoshi Nakamatsu.

Lazarus turned away from the offerings the scientists proffered him—flavored water to dispel the tastes of the things they gave him—and continued to listen to their conversation as they worked. As they worked on him.

Their gossip intrigued him. It was one of the various ways he gathered information. They were a mix of men and women of various ages. They hastened their movement with ease of their surroundings and the work they were performing. Collecting samples from his body, looking under microscopes and deftly handling sharps. Though the air vents provided adequate air circulation, the room felt stuffy, which stank with too many human and chemical scents mingling.

"Odd how the sombra have been behaving, lately."said one of the laboratory workers.

"Yeah and have you heard about the riots down in the lower cities? The people are afraid." said another.

"Those weren't riots, just some upset farmers that had to destroy half of their livestock because the undead infected them. The meat had to be incinerated."

"Ok, but if the sombra aren't put under control soon, we will see riots. Where do you think our food comes from? There are no farms up here. We get all of our food from down below."

"Doubt we'll be affected as much as those down below. People will riot when they can't put food on the table for their families."

"They'll eventually be as big as the rebellion that is

starting in the west. I hear it's because the lord emperor won't do something about the sombra over there, either."

"I heard it's because of the tariffs he is subjugating those people."

"That is definitely part of the problem, but the main problem is the undead. The people call them hada over there."

"Down below, everyone is afraid to go out at night. I can't imagine what the western kingdoms feel right now. I heard they have a lot more undead over there than we do here."

"And the monks continue to spout rubbish. Prayer this. Action that. None of it works for those people. Soon they'll be asking of it here. It's scientifically implausible."

"But not impossible. It hasn't been disproven, yet."

"It seems like it. The sombra just keep coming…"

"Shhhhh, we aren't supposed to talk about any of that, here." The woman who spoke had long dark hair and light blue eyes, a trait that was a rarity as Lazarus had not seen many people with skin like hers or eyes like that. The woman was reading through some documents, her eyes narrowed at whatever she saw. Lazarus saw the two female lab workers bow to her before falling into silence.

He did not let them know that he was listening to them, that he heard every word they whispered.

Unlike the other specimens that moaned and cried out in front of the scientist—some even begging for them to stop—Lazarus sat quietly as his arm was filled with bright blue liquids every day. Cool liquid flooded his veins that took his breath away, casting gooseflesh over his skin, his muscles rippled with the effect quickly replaced by a heat that promised to burn him for hours. Sharp pain shot through his arm, down into his spine, down into his legs—his toes flexed and stretched at odd angles—before the sharpness, the fire, shot up to his brain.

"Sit back, and it will go easier for you." A hand on his forehead coaxed him to lay backwards. He always complied when they spoke to him. It had been the brown-haired scientist.

Arrrggh—why must there always be pain?

"I feel sorry for him and the others."

"Don't be. He isn't even human." A man's voiced said as he rifled through papers.

"Looks like an ordinary boy to me," the voice said kindly and full of pity. The hand withdrew from his head and brown-haired scientist moved away.

"Don't go thinking that way. Or you might grow feelings for him and his kind."

"Can't help it. He looks like he isn't even older than six or seven. I have a nephew around that age."

"His chart says he is six. Tall for his age, though. But not human. He doesn't even respond to the treatments he is given. Not like some others." The balding man stared at him for a moment before returning to something that caught his interest in the document he was reading.

Pain, white hot pain pulsed down his spine and into his chest. Each breath came in sharp bursts of agony. Ughh… He tried to control the motion of his head lolling on his shoulders and was grateful to be sitting back.

"I have to wear earplugs, or I get nothing done," another voice chimed in. "I can't stand the cries."

"Do what you have to do to get the job done. Professor Yoshi Nakamatsu doesn't like incompetents."

"No, I don't think he does." The woman with the dark hair spoke. "You all might just want to get back to work." Her blue eyes glanced at him from above the documents she was holding. He did not let her know that he had been watching her.

"If it helps at all," the man spoke. "just remember he isn't human. Doesn't feel the same way as you and I do. Or your nephew. Remember that." Unlike the scientist with light skin and blue eyes, this man was of medium build and average appearance. A balding head that might have once held dark hair and a light tan skin. A native to Gestahl. Like many of the imperial staff and those who lived in the upper city, he might have been related, a hundred times removed, from the lord emperor's line.

Lazarus looked at his own flesh. Pale. Sickly white except for the bright blue veins that he could see spider webbing from the back of his hands and down his arms, to beneath the garb he wore. He had seen his own appearance only a handful of times before. He did not look similar to those of the laboratory staff. He had only ever seen a few people with skin like his and eyes almost the same lightness as his own. Using his special awareness that he knew was his alone, he could sense that the scientist was not ill. Did not harbor a darkness inside of her… like he did.

Arrrggh...

The pain inside his skull thrummed just as someone grabbed at him, thumb placed over his wrist.

Was this what my life will be? Is this how I am going to die? He would never know the answers to his existence. Never know why he was here... or the wrongness of it all.

No!

Lazarus began to fall into the blackness, the void, that was his mind. His head rolling on his shoulders. He could feel the finger on his skin, a sensation of spiders crawling up his arm. He wanted to move away from their touch; he wanted to flee. His skin felt an invisible resistance. It would be no use. He could not get away. The scientists were everywhere. He turned his head away from the glancing eyes of the one who touched him and managed to gasp without attracting attention. He felt the tickle of sweat bead and roll down the side of his face with the effort of keeping his pain a secret.

"Finish up with him," the scientist said. A memory came to his mind, a time when he had been in the corridor... her name was Sierra. "Put him in his cell. His samples won't be changing. He is perfect. We have other children that we need to look at." A grimace crossed her mouth, as though she had tasted a particular bitter tasting concoction.

"Excited to see that woman and her child?" It was that male staff member speaking again.

"Rishu, I like to make sure that she and the babe receive proper treatment when Nakamatsu and Doctor Axel are not pestering them."

"What is that supposed to mean?" Rishu said.

"How it sounds. They're two seagulls fighting over food."

"Food? Food?" he repeated himself.

"Precious food. Rare food. One of a kind, types. They're obsessed. Someone's got to make sure the mother and child are tended to properly."

The man crossed his arms. "It sounds like you have something to say. Out with it."

"There is nothing to say. There is nothing to add. Just the facts."

"If Professor Yoshi Nakamatsu heard you say this, he would—"

"He would what? Have me flogged? Mistreat me like he does to his poor assistant Karyn?" Sierra said.

"You have no right to speak like that," Rishu said.

With a flick of her hand, the file closed, and she slipped the documents beneath her arm. "Don't I? Well then— better go run along and report me. He knows where to find me if he wants to disabuse me of my mind."

Rishu glared at her and then he strode away, out the door, down the evenly tiled path, his short legs carrying him rather hastily out of sight. Faintly, Lazarus thought he heard footsteps quicken into a run.

"You've made yourself an enemy," one assistant nearby said. "Be careful, Sierra."

"He is vile and full of envy. Nearly as bad as the professor."

"Can't please all the sycophants," said one of the female lab workers.

Sierra's mouth thinned to a line. "And that is why

they're called sycophants. But I'd like to call them, suck ups."

"Is it true about what you said about... about the two heads of departments fighting over the Athaian and her baby?"

Sierra crossed her arms. "I'm afraid it's true. The good doctor, praise his name, means no harm but his pestering is harming the woman almost as much as Nakamatsu's. Sometimes a new mom just needs peace and relative quiet."

"You'd think she gets enough of that when she is alone in the cell with her baby."

"That's right," one of the lab personnel said. "Didn't she just give birth in the small hours of the morning?"

"Yes, that is correct."

"Ought to count her blessings she is even allowed to be with the babe right now. I am sure the professor and Doctor Axel would love to study the child and the mother more than they already do."

Sierra smiled a tight-lipped smile but did not respond. Instead, she moved closer to Lazarus but not close enough to make him become wary of her. The research staff began to whisper mundane things that Lazarus did not keep track of, instead he only had eyes for the woman. She also seemed to ignore all the small talk. He watched her as she looked over the samples but by the fixed smile on her face and the look in her eyes, he could tell that her thoughts were not on the data.

Cool hands touched his throat and he blinked slowly, his eyes and inner lids feeling dry and unused. "He's recovering well. A remarkable specimen."

"That he is. A very special boy."

"I'll take him to his room, Sierra. Go check on that mother and the child." The way she said it left no doubt who Sierra would go check on. But it left him wondering, just who was this woman and child and why were they so important? *More important than me?*

"If it pleases you, special one," the research staff said. "please stand."

Lazarus sat up, standing on shaky legs that he did not let on to the staff how debilitated he felt. A few of the lab technicians formed around him and they started down the corridor, passing work stations and unused procedure rooms with a variety of tech. The lab personnel watched Lazarus as if they knew he was well broke to the invisible collars they had placed around his neck.

He left that room with only two of the scientists providing his escort.

4

TSUSKE

Tsuske walked the streets of the upper city, the capital of the empire; Gestahl. He stepped down into the streets and from their brightness, into the darkness of an alley. How had the sombra gotten up here? His breath puffed out in front of him, and his feet could feel the chill of the ground. The soft footsteps behind him the only indication that his squad were near.

They strode together, through the alley carrying light arsenal, and a small covered cage with a wounded animal within it. Each of them carried a cage on their back, strapped in like a pack. They didn't want to attract the notice of the civilians in the streets; people would know what an injured or sick animal meant. They covered the cage so that the masses did not surmise the purpose of COBRA lurking about in the shadows if their eyes found them. For the upper city, the people were unused to such grotesque sights and the sight could cause a panic. But for a sombra, a covered cage would not prevent the creatures from knowing what lay within. They could sense sickness. They could sense death.

Just what we want...

"I'll take the north and eastern part of the city," Tsuske said. "Nileen, you take south. Dmytro, you take west."

"Got it," Dmytro said.

"Why could we not have enlisted more COBRA for this?" Nileen asked.

"As I said during the briefing, we should not let too many know of this," he said. "And besides, the other squads are busy. We cannot pull them from their own assignments."

"They're COBRA. They ought to know." Nileen persisted.

"I agree and they will. But this is important. We need to find the sombra immediately, and we do not want to distract the others from their important tasks."

"Let it go, Nileen." Dmytro said. "The sooner we are done with this task, the sooner we can go get a drink."

"Save thoughts like that for after the mission," Tsuske said.

They split apart without another word.

I hope it does not rain, he thought. It was still morning, but the cloud cover made it seem later in the day than it was. Winter in Gestahl rarely had flurries of the soft downfall of snow, instead cloud layering and rain accompanied by heavy winds was the usual climate this time of year. In Higaz, the kingdom of his birth, the climate would experience all four seasons, here in Gestahl, there only seemed to be two seasons, both comprising of one major weather; clouds.

He sniffed the air, trying to catch any suspicious scents, and only caught the fragrance of bakeries and distant restaurants, mingled with the soft scent of perfume from the nearby gardens. The upper city was clean, the streets without debris, the buildings refined. Along each street there were gardens and covered furrows for water and ridges for plant life to grow. The people of Gestahl fancied ornamental plants. Each tier of the city had its own favorites. Each district governed by a Great House, and the people within those neighboring streets favored the flowers and plants of the highborn. It was a way of honoring them, a way to show who they supported and which line they had originally come from. Flowers and favored exotic animals. No one would mix between the classes. Those born from the lineage of the white buck would not hang ornate decorations for the red fox or the black boar. Gardens reflected the Great Houses, head lady's favored flora.

The city was organized.

The number of people passing through the streets slackened as the sky promised rain. It was just Tsuske and the lonely, empty backstreets. He began to wonder if he was looking in the wrong places. Thinking he could lure the sombra away from any hidden illness that a citizen would try to hide from the lord emperor and any of the great family lines.

Maybe I need to go to a more public place. A place where people congregate. An area where there could be the sick or the injured and such a place could be covered up. Hidden in plain sight.

He moved out from the back streets, stepping foot into the brightly lit neighborhoods, passing bountiful gardens with large plants shadowed by the buildings that were dozens of stories high. He looked up, glancing at all the small and large balconies, lavish with decorations and ornaments. The Great houses; their families and apartments of the citizens.

With his COBRA cloak on, he veiled his face with its large hood, passing amongst the civilians with little notice, though some did cast their eyes to his back. There would be nothing for it. Tsuske was entering the livelier part of the city; the market places.

Leaving behind the refined looks of the Great Houses and the wealth of their families and people governed beneath them, the marketplace had sprung up shockingly fast, in defiance to the whispers of a sombra lurking in the streets. The people were resilient and would overcome the obstacles that jumped out at them.

Winter festivities were getting under way. Today was the mark of a new year and on the second day of every year, the people celebrated—every day of the week. The emperor encouraged it. Tsuske wondered if the monks would send an inquiry to anyone who had missed the day of prayer and the day of giving's because of the whispers of an undead on the streets. Few would forego listening to the sermons that the monks delivered on the first day of every year.

He walked down the main thoroughfare with shops

along each side, preparing for tonight's festivities. Shanties and tents propped up with Grotton made brewery, bakeries and foodstuffs and goods for sale. It was one of the few times per year that the lord emperor permitted Grotton goods from Grotton sellers. Guards stood nearby overseeing the shopkeepers, some were patrolling the streets; everything was carefully regulated.

Nearby a group of musicians were starting a melancholy tune, ballads would be sung tonight, courtier bards would become street gleeman during the festivities and would recant the humbling words of their forefathers and the righteous directive from the monks. There would be music, drinks and dancing. For so long as the streets remained civil.

The Gestahlian born merchants had rebelled, complaining about lack of storage space or the need to be closer to one shop or a wall, or a garden. Which incited some civilians to gather and protest the previous day. Fingers pointed at the lower-class rabble from the Grotto being allowed to participate, allowed to take up space. Then word was passed around about a sombra and the Athaian being captured. In reality, the Gestahlian born just wanted a larger market that was harder to regulate while the Grottons just wanted to sell their goods. To be seen by the higher people and to feed their families from the profits of selling their wares. Regardless, it had caused a bit of an uproar. The lord emperor had threatened to shut down the winter festivities—an act that Tsuske was sure that would not have a positive impact. People relied on the festivities, the holidays to sell their wares outside of the normal day-to-day grind of a marketplace.

Merchants from all the family lines were mixed in on the main thoroughfare outside of the Imperial tramways. Tsuske passed three different bakeries in a row; he had never understood why merchants selling the same things always congregated. Wouldn't it be better to set up where you did not have as much competition?

He moved along the tents and canvasses; the shop keepers eying him before tending to their business. Tsuske did not feel comfortable out in the open. The marketplace was empty now. People still tending to the monk's speeches at the Speaker's Podium—soon, though, the marketplace will grow like an overgrown reaper's vine, snaring everyone in its path. The streets will be congested with the influx of people. Tramways unloading a flood of people.

Tsuske made his way to the market districts central well: a large, round ornate pond with sculpture figures spouting fresh water. In the summer, this area would attract a lot of young children. Today and for a week straight; it attracted hoisted tents and canvass walls. The fragrance of strong brew and hard alcohol and piss would wade through the crowds, alerting everyone where the drinking pavilions were located.

He heard voices coming from the nearest erect tent.

The first bar that he chose was inside a large tent. It already smelled of spilled beer and sweaty bodies—the drunks always came early. Men and women laughed. Tonight, all the taverns in the area would no doubt fill up, people would use over turned crates as tables and chairs when the other seating arrangements were taken. He spied people who wore regular labor worker clothing—not highborn or upper Gestahl worker uniforms. These men and women had come from the Grotto, labor workers hired to do a lot of the physical work that nobody from the upper city could be bothered to perform. Such menial tasks suited those who were used to it. And labor workers would have heard or seen things.

Tsuske looked around, at the other tents that had been erected, this area would be filling up fast. He could already see another set of musicians' coming to claim territory. A large open space was left unused for those who would wish to dance with the merriment. His eyes fell back to the tent flap that had been pulled open, inviting. This was a low-end tavern, and likely had the only occupants in the area.

Still, this seemed a good place as any to begin his investigation in the rumors of a sombra. If any undead lurked in the area, it would find him and the dying beast that he carried on his back. He entered.

The bar comprised of stacked boxes—too poor to have proper tables and seating arrangements, though the chairs and tables present were occupied with workers. Tsuske walked in, casually and took a seat near the entrance. An old man with greying hair looked at him and looked at the square covered "box" that he had set on the ground. He hoped the man took it for a workman's supplies.

"No pets in here, sir. This is a drinking establishment, unless you plan on getting whatever little thing in there, drunk."

Ah—no sign of getting off that easily, Tsuske thought.

"It's a canary, don't worry about it."

"A canary? A bird?" The barkeeper look at him suspiciously, this caused a few of the other patrons—labor workers—to turn and look at him and his package with interest.

"Yes, a bird old man. Got a problem with a little bird?"

The man frowned at him. "I guess I got nothing wrong with a little bird. You from the mines, then?"

Tsuske grunted and shrugged.

"Well—as you can see, we aren't exactly open yet. But seeing you are one of the laborer's, you might as well have a drink. What do you want?" the old man asked.

"Whatever you have that is warm but not room temperature."

"We have sake."

"That will be fine."

A barmaid came and gave him his drink. "Do you want something to eat?"

Tsuske shook his head and he paid with three bronze coins. He watched her move away. He saw that a few of the other patrons were staring at him. A table of three, two men and a woman, they were playing a game of cards. Their eyes were not on the game.

He picked up the sake, the steam coming from the choko; a ceramic cup that held warm drinks. Sniffing at the soft fragrance of fermented rice, it smelled clean and not stale, he took his first sip. The flavor was all right for where it came from. Down in the Grotto, it was not unheard of to be served stale sake—or old fermented stuff that only slightly resembled it. He took another sip and sighed as if he had been working down in the mines. He knew that he did not have much of an appearance of one who had been working down there—but he would not argue with another person's perception.

"Have you heard about the sombra?" A woman's voice asked.

"There has been some talk, more like whispers, from the toppers about seeing them up here."

"As if their lives are going to be ruined by the little devils. They're harmless," she said, and he could sense the mocking in her voice. "They're just full mischief. They're confused. They're misunderstood." A couple of the other patrons laughed.

"Hey don't mock them. Quetzal, didn't you say you saw one of the things earlier today?"

"I did. Saw where it went. Done near scared the piss out of me."

"Hey where are you going?"

A shadow moved to his side, and he glanced up to see the man who had been looking at him had come over; lifting a crate and sitting it next to him. It was the man who had been speaking with the two.

"You could have brought your chair. There is no need to sit on a crate," Tsuske said.

"Nah—I don't know if I'll like being over here. Too close to the tent flap. There's a chill in the air, ya know?"

"I know."

"Sake, huh? I prefer myself a good hard ale."

"I wanted something warm."

"You could have gotten hard cider."

"Do I look like a woman to you?" Tsuske asked, putting a little heat in his voice. "Or a boy?"

"No, man. No." The guy sat on his seat, elbows on the table as he eyed Tsuske. He didn't say anything more until the woman he had been playing cards with spoke.

"Quetzal, leave him be. He obviously doesn't want to talk to you, do you, sweetheart?" Tsuske looked at her and a hint of a smile danced on her face before she took another sip of her ale. "Oh, Quetzal, I think you're barking up the wrong tree."

The man, Quetzal, sighed and made to get up and leave. "Wait," Tsuske said. "You don't have to go. I don't mind if you want to drink with me. Sit."

"You sure?" he hesitated.

Tsuske nodded his head, trying to put a smile to his face, unsure if he had succeeded. But the man did not seem to be discouraged from whatever he saw. The look of uncertainty passed, and he sat back down.

"Oh, maybe I am wrong. Maybe luck is on your side tonight, Quetzal. A new year, a new fling." Tsuske saw her wink—it was directed at him. He was not sure what was going on, but maybe he could use it to his advantage. He pretended to not see that the man's cheeks as they flamed with embarrassment.

"So," he began. "What do you do?" He took another sip of sake, the choko warm against his fingers.

"I'm a planter. A field worker. Though my family has a sow and we sell piglets on occasion—pig milk, too." He shrugged and drank from his tanker. He sat there a moment, looking unsure again. Then his eyes lifted from the amber liquid and looked, not at him, but the sake in his hands. "You sure you're a miner?"

His hands. They weren't gloved and would not appear as a miner's hands. Shit.

"No," Tsuske said and saw that the man, Quetzal, had smiled at his answer. I can't interrogate too hard to get my answer, less I attract notice, he thought. If I seem too ignorant, these people will grow suspicious. He decided to try a different approach with this man. "Not anymore a mine worker is a mine worker without a mine, as a baker is a baker who does not have yeast to bake his breads."

The barkeeper worked behind his improvised bar. A couple guards poked their heads into the room, and Tsuske felt their eyes fall on him before leaving. They would watch this area heavily as the day wore into night.

"Is it true?" The woman at the table asked. She leaned forward, interest in her eyes. "Is it true about the mines? How is everyone dealing with the cease in production?"

Tsuske frowned and looked at his clean gloved hands. He knew that production had slowed because of the undead blocking the tunnels—but cease? Is that what the word on the street was?

"Vera," Quetzal said. "Don't say things like that." Quetzal rubbed his eyes. "I'm really sorry. She isn't normally so…"

"Vera-bose?" Tsuske asked.

"Chatty." Quetzal flashed him a hesitant smile. "I'm sorry about the mines. It must be tough. Especially with all the layoffs. I've seen many mine workers carrying their caged canary around down stairs. Can't help but feel sorry for them." Downstairs. He meant the Grotto. He felt rough hands across his knuckles, and he looked up. *Oh sweet Mosiaen,* Tsuske thought. *He's flirting with me.*

"Why is it he gets off easy but not me?" Vera pouted, but she looked anything but saddened by the prospect. Tsuske could sense the humor melting off of her. Her smile said all.

"Leave them be," the man next to her said.

"Oh, Fenrir. Finny-finny-fanny-finster." She emptied the rest of her ale into her mouth, swaying in her seat.

"Vera, you're drunk," Quetzal said, chuckling. He removed his hand from the back of Tsuske's and drank from his tanker, setting it down empty. "Barmaid? Another, please?" Three copper coins hit the table. Then he looked over at Tsuske, a sympathetic smile on his face. "And another sake, please."

"Sure thing, boys," the barmaid said from across the tent said.

That was how he began his night, and how it led to disaster.

5

TSUSKE

Three empty choko cups sat in front of him. The last one was still warm. Vera-bose was chatting with Quetzal while Fenrir sat quietly, looking at his hands. He was not much of a speaker. Tsuske liked that about him.

"So…" Vera-bose said as she grimaced at the mug of plain water that Quetzal had convinced her to drink. She sipped at it as though it went down her gullet like acid.

"It's not that bad, Ver-Ver!" Quetzal said. The man, not much older than a boy, looked at Tsuske. He seemed to be the only one to catch his smile. "I'll buy your next drink."

"Then, get me another." She rested her head on her hand, looking miserable. And not for the amount of drinks she had consumed. "The men in here are all ugly." She sighed and then grimaced sheepishly. "Not you guys— you're not ugly. Ugh… you know what I mean."

"Vera, maybe it's time to get you something to eat," Fenrir said into his cards.

"I'm not hungry. I need me some love. It's the New Year!

The second day of the new year will be upon us soon." She sighed again, "I should have gone to the monk's sermons. I'll be audited, just you wait and see. They'll find out who did not show, or the damn rats will tell them. I'm a cobbler's apprentice. I work with my Uncle when he isn't at the tannery. I can't afford to be ticketed."

"None of us went," Fenrir said. "We are labor workers. They won't expect us all to go."

"He has a point," Quetzal said. "I mean, look at us. Would you want us to go to a holy place looking like this?" He pointed at the dust on his tunic and grimaced with disgust. "I've been hauling things all day."

Maybe it was the sombra on his mind, maybe it was the humid atmosphere, the dim lights. Or maybe it was the alcohol speaking but Tsuske felt himself speak. "The monks don't expect any of the lowborn to go, though some come to their talks. The lowborn ones only think of themselves." Tsuske knew the words were the wrong thing to say as soon as they came out of his mouth.

Quetzal looked at him, confused. He looked about to laugh at a joke, one that he did not find funny. Fenrir only looked at him.

"What the hell does that mean, Serjeesh?"

Tsuske coughed into his hand. That was the name he had given them when small talk forced him to give them pleasantries in return. "It's not what I say. It's what they say."

Her eyes narrowed at him. "Who's they?"

Quetzal opened his mouth and then closed it. He looked like he wanted to speak, to defend him, perhaps, but he did not. The barkeep came by the table, when the barmaids were preoccupied to collect the empty bottles, and he gave Tsuske a certain look. And nodded.

Is my cover blown? He felt his heart flutter, but he played it cool and did not respond to the gesture.

He cleared his throat. "The imperials..." Another wrong thing to say, he knew it. "You know... it's how they treat us. We got to do what we have to do to survive, whether we want to. Whether we care. It's all the same." He felt his heart stir at his own words. Did he really believe it?

This earned a look from Fenrir, comprehension and sympathy shown in his eyes. He nodded and put down his cards. Quietly he said, "Everybody has been mistreated by the toppers. But we should not talk about it, Serj."

Oh light... he was starting to feel sick. He'd only downed three choko cups of sake, yes, but they were little cups. He blinked and turned when he felt Quetzal's hands on him again.

I'm not going to be able to imitate this, he groaned inwardly. *But if I dont, I won't be able to get the answers I need.* His body leaning away from the other man, hesitant. Not unless I live in this moment, be part of this moment. Just as Quetzal looked disappointed, Tsuske leaned towards him. He could feel his hands shaking. There was a tremor in his knees that he could not shake off.

What is wrong with me?

Feeling the need to be moving he asked, "Do you want to get out of here?"

A smile spread across Quetzal's face, brightening he said, "you sure?"

"The air is stuffy. Too many people in here. Maybe we can get a beer somewhere, just you and I?"

He made to stand and then, purposely, moved a little too fast—at least he thought it was intentional—when his hand tried to seize the pitcher in the middle of the table, knocking the thing over. It had been half drained and nearly missed spoiling the table as the pitcher went shooting across the bar, hitting the side of the dark canvass flap near the barkeeper's makeshift bar table. His face immediately grew warm. The alcohol had hit him, hard. The barkeeper stared at him, eyebrows furrowed. Tsuske stared right back at him. Something was not right about that man. He stared too openly; his eyes too full of knowing that it irritated him. He moved towards the older man and noticed the man was dressed oddly for a barkeeper… then a hand grabbed his arm, steadying him and pulling him closer.

"This way, the tent flap is this way."

He turned and shoved Quetzal away. "Don't touch me, I can walk. I can do it." He swayed slightly, looking around the ground for the brown cover that contained the cage. "I need to get the critter." He was very aware that the man had nearly touched some weapons he carried on his person. He had not intended for that to happen.

"I can do that for you," Quetzal reached down and grabbed at the straps.

"No, no. I got it. Just back up a bit." He grabbed at the straps and hoisted it none too gently onto his back. Quetzal gave him space, but he did not seem deterred by the roughness of Tsuske's voice.

The barkeeper was all too pleased to see them going, though he did not say it. Then a bouncer appeared at the tent flap. Tsuske had known that the man was there. He seemed to know Quetzal as he gave him a nod of greetings and said, "Another one? You got a collection or something?"

At his side, Quetzal shrugged but tried to eye Tsuske sideways, to see if he had heard or understood what the man had meant—or cared at what was said. Tsuske pretended to the latter. He glanced at Quetzal and smiled encouragingly. It was a weird thing on his face, he knew it and was glad that none but a civilian saw it.

"The night is still young, who knows what will come?" Quetzal smiled back at him.

THEY STEPPED out into the night, which was filled with dazzling lights, lit torches, and decorations that esteemed the festivities. Crowds of people, were all around them. Music played and the square—the open court—had been filled with moving, dancing bodies. Along the streets and the tents and shops they passed, people danced in place, they drank where they ought not to, and ate sitting or standing where they could find space. Kids ran around, chasing one another, a stray dog, or chickens or pigs that had been loosed for the festivities. Later—much later— during the daylight hours, the neighborhoods would gather their children and there would be daily hunts for the loosed animals, whoever caught them, won prizes, though the wealthy did not care about the prize. It was the symbol of the hunt that mattered to these people, the pride to be the ones to have captured the loosed beasties.

Quetzal walked with a youthful spry in his step. Tsuske could tell that the man was around his age, if not a year younger. His face was angular but soft where it should be, with a small scar on his chin. "How did you get that scar?"

"Oh this?" He pointed at his chin. "I work with some sows at a pig farm. They can be quite bitey."

"One bit you?"

He shook his head. "No, but one did bite my leg. I took a fall and hit my face in the side of her pen. Some workers saw me and helped pull me away from her. They say I am lucky she didn't find flesh; pigs are known to develop a taste for people. I say I am lucky I didn't land in manure I had been cleaning up." Quetzal paused, as if expecting something from him. "What are you doing while the mines are effected by the sombra?"

"What do you mean, what am I doing?"

"Well, if that was me, no job would mean no money. My father would beat me until I found work or sell me to the tower."

"You're too old to be sold to the tower, unwillingly."

"Well… yeah. That's true. But my father would find a way. He doesn't like me too much. Not since I turned down the woman he had arranged for me to marry."

Tsuske frowned. "Fathers can be like that, sometimes." He remembered his own father… an honorable man, but hard. Disciplined.

"It wasn't the first time, either. He tried to find me a

woman four or five times. I could tell with the last one he wasn't even trying anymore."

"Why do you say that?"

"For starters, he bought a pretty dress, something my sisters might like, and dressed up an old sow we had purchased for piglets."

Tsuske laughed at that. Quetzal smiled and launched into another story. Forgetting the original question that he had asked. Keep him talking, he thought. Keep him from asking questions.

The evening was growing darker. They had left the festivities and the people all behind them, though music seemed to follow them; the sad tale of a melody on the wind. Tsuske led Quetzal away from all the people. He would get the answers he needed. He knew that his teammates had been unsuccessful as they had not contacted him.

It's now or never, he thought. *Sometimes, in order to do good, you have to be bad.* A phrase that Director Voren had told him once.

Tsuske looked up. There had been no rain, not yet. High above he could see some stars as the striated clouds parted to reveal the void of the night sky. Were there gods up there staring down at him? Weighing his actions and judging him for them? He looked at Quetzal. The man had stopped speaking, glancing at him. *What... what had he been saying?* Following him was getting harder as his mind drifted with the clouds.

"Go on," Tsuske said.

Quetzal smiled, grabbing his hand, pulling Tsuske to a full stop. *Damn it, what had I missed?*

He shouldn't have found it so surprising. Quetzal had been showing him favor. Tsuske had come alone into the tavern and while he would not describe himself as gorgeous, some might describe him as "cute", though he wasn't exactly ugly. His blood though, it was foul and darker than anything this boy saw in him. He was Higaziit. Born to traitors.

Sometimes, in order to do good, you have to be bad.

He looked into Quetzal's face, young and full of youthful innocence. But not too innocent—he remembered what he had said to the bouncer. Then he pulled out his gun and stuck the end to the man's throat.

6

TSUSKE

A torch flickered on the wall nearby, and Tsuske shoved the gun into the neck of the man in front of him. He could smell the man's sweat, the fear and lust, mixed with the pungent scent of oil from the torch. Stupid decorative torches. Makra powered the city, such torches were archaic and only for show. *What was the point? Looking pretty? Give the people a sense of what... a passing of time? A sense of a lack of technology?* Only in the Grotto did many places still have need for fire lit torches; districts furthest from the central spiral would be more primitive and have less technology.

At a glare from Quetzal, Tsuske smiled and relented the pressure just a little. He took a step back, gun still on alert. A cry echoed down the street. He paused, listening, never turning from the man he pointed his gun at. He seemed to sense Tsuske's resolve and, in utter shock, remained in place, still and absolutely quiet.

Good, it will go easier this way.

The shouts of merriment died, moving away to enjoy the festivities elsewhere, in a more lit and livelier part of the city, no doubt. Or perhaps moving further away after glancing at two men who's bodies were very close. Something in Tsuske stirred, but he hissed it down. The man that was the focus of his weapon let out a quivering breath.

Tsuske stood there, and as the seconds ticked on to a minute. Then two minutes. The shock of the moment ebbed, being replaced with anger. He could sense Quetzal's anger beginning to rise. Quetzal was not the type of person to be taken advantage of. He might have been a year, maybe two, younger than Tsuske, but he was larger. He was a man who got what he wanted.

"What are you doing with a gun, Serjeesh? Is Serjeesh even your actual name? My gods, what're you going to do with me?"

Tsuske almost laughed. For one who had a gun held to him, he sure did ask a lot of questions. "I will ask you a question. I expect you to answer." He paused, waiting for the man to curse, to spew hatred, to acknowledge the position he was in. He did none of those things. He just stared back at him, and blinked. "The sombra you saw in the city earlier, where did it go?"

"The sombra? The undead? Why do you want to know?"

"Answer me!" Quetzal just stood there in utter disbelief. Tsuske did not want to use force, but he would if Quetzal did not speak soon.

"I don't know. I saw it earlier at the unloading docks and then in the garden square between Houses; boar, ram, buck and goat. The gardens, it was attracted to something in the gardens."

"Is this a joke to you?" Tsuske said, the barrel of his 9mm pointing right between Quetzal's eyes.

"Look, Serj—"

Tsuske slammed the butt of the gun into the side of the man's face. He hit the wall, sliding to the ground, eyes blinking rapidly as his head spun. He looked up at him, his hand cradling his face. Blood dripped from a busted lip. There would be bruises to tell by morning. Quetzal spat, spraying phlegm and blood onto Tsuske's shoes.

Tsuske took a couple steps back, disgusted.

"Why are you doing this?" Quetzal demanded. "Is it the sombra you're interested in? Why are you interested in it?" Then his eyes, as if remembering something, slid to Tsuske's back and what hid beneath the covering, and then they widened with comprehension. "You're not a miner."

"No, I'm not."

"What're you going to do with me?" Quetzal looked afraid now. Very afraid. He had crossed the path of a very terrifying creature. A creature of the empire. The empire's serpent. Something seen as more loathsome than a mere walking spirit.

Tsuske leaned in and pulled Quetzal to his feet, handgun still ready when abruptly, a group of people came sauntering down the street. Tsuske knew that they were young—teenagers—heading back home or to cause mischief elsewhere, away from the crowds the festivities brought. Several of the kids glanced at the two men and began to giggle, which caught the other's attention. Heat rushed to Tsuske's cheeks when he realized what they might have thought they saw.

He watched the teens disappear around the corner, and he realized that had been a mistake. Maybe it had been the drinks that day that left his mind a little too numb, maybe it was the loss of his helicopter STINGRAY, maybe it was the hint of ginseng and pine that permeated up from Quetzal's body. For just the briefest of moments, he had been distracted. Like the wings of a butterfly, a gentle flutter touched the side of his neck, startling him, but not before the warmth of Quetzal's breath sent heat through his body.

He turned and back handed Quetzal in the face with his gun again—which he promptly fell to the ground. Tsuske pulled out his dagger and pressed it into the man's stomach, not enough to kill, not enough to wound, but just enough to immobilize the man. If he moved even the slightest, he would be impaled.

His comm unit went off in his ear, and he glared at Quetzal who's mouth broke into a rictus grin, blood trailing down from two breaks in his swollen lips. He would definitely be bruised by morning. He sheathed the dagger, not caring to use it more than he needed to and pressed his earpiece as his eyes caught movement down the street—getting nearer.

Something shadowy moved down the corridor and then broke off to the left, down a small alley, small walking path parallel to the garden path.

Quetzal had seen something in the gardens. Something

that looked to be interested in the gardens. What would be interesting in the gardens besides plant life? And then it dawned on him. The festivities.

"Pig farmer?" He asked.

Taken by surprise, Quetzal was slow to respond. "No, I'm a field worker."

"You said your father had a sow; you sell piglets."

"That's right. He does, not me. I do little with the sow as I already work in the field and with the animals in the corrals."

"Did your father sell his piglets yesterday or today?"

"What?"

"Answer the question."

"Yeah—maybe. I don't know."

"When did you see the sombra, was it earlier today?"

"I've already told you. I saw it earlier today, twice. At the unloading docks of the tramway and by the garden square in the—"

"Yeah, I remember." He looked down at the man, who had remained on the ground. "Get out of here."

"What?"

"Are you as stupid as you look? I told you to leave. Go or I will kill you."

Quetzal swallowed hard, but he hesitated. Tsuske took a step back, never turning his gun away from him. With his gun hand, he motioned the man to flee. With quick reflexes, he stood on wobbly legs and ran down the street, back towards the festivities—to other people—without looking back.

Tsuske ran—he had no time to answer the comm unit as he dashed after the ominous figure—his black cloak fluttering behind him.

7

TSUSKE

A shadow loped up ahead, moving unnaturally fast. A memory from the power plant came to mind and he quickened his pace. Tsuske needed to attract the creature's notice, but from the looks of it, the undead had already been distracted. Preoccupied, something had attracted its attention. As he ran, he put his gun into its holster beneath his cloak.

How can something dead look that much like a person in the dark? His ear piece vibrated with comm signal and he pressed his index finger to the sensor.

"Tsuske, do you read?" It was Nileen's voice.

"Tsuske here," he panted into the earpiece.

"Are you running?"

"Found the sombra," he said.

"Oh good, I was wondering why you had not picked up the first time—wait... what? Why are you running? Is it chasing you?"

"No, it's not chasing me. It is chasing something else."

"Where are you located?"

"Northeastern district, between the neighborhoods—away from the festivals."

"You were at one of the district's festivals?"

"No time, can't talk right now. My head is still swooning. I need to catch up to the thing and distract it."

"We're on our way."

And the comm went silent.

We? Were Dmytro and Nileen together? No time for those questions, he thought. *I need to get to the thing before it catches whatever it is chasing or worse—accidently kills it and then claims its body as a host.*

He ran into open gardens. Empty. He either lost his quarry somewhere back down the garden pathway between the neighboring walls and the garden, or it had disappeared again, a talent the sombra were known for.

Or there was nothing there in the first place, a part of his mind worried. I have not been thinking straight of late.

Why? What changed? His mind raced back through the last thirty-six hours. A lot had changed. Starting with the loss of STINGRAY. Then the capture of the damned woman.

He walked around the edge of the circular garden. Small walls of marble and stone, keeping the flora contained. The cobblestone ground was free of debris. The land keepers tended to the gardens very well. He could feel the air moving through the plants before he heard the rustling of leaves.

Tsuske noted the faint light emanating from a bush, up ahead—no, not from within it, but from between the branches and the leaves. Festivity lights shun dazzling, that alternated between warm and cool colors, giving the bushes a paranormal glow. With it, the sound of people in a low, echoing clatter.

He moved along the bush, moving to the next set of trees, to the next opening and the pathway through the garden when something caught his attention. A giggle, a soft sigh and a squeal of a wounded animal. Turning back to the colorful bush, he peered through the leaves and out into the street.

Four teenagers, three boys and one girl, stood underneath the lamppost. One boy was doing something odd in the back, jumping and falling to the ground, creating a chorus of laughter from the girl and one of the other boys. Tsuske eyes fell on the lone boy, the one that was crouching low, no not crouching, he was sitting on something and holding part of it in his hands. Movement, the color of flesh, wiggled beneath that boy's grasp, but his hands were like iron claws that held whatever it was steady. Tsuske watched as the boy bent one of the creature's legs at an odd angle, causing the animal to squeal out in pain. Its loud cry echoing down the street as its three other legs scraped effortlessly against the cobblestone.

Along the wall, not too far from the boy, squatted a dark, menacing shape, staring hungrily at the boy who had the injured animal. His eyes fell to the boy jumping on top of the undead creature, before sliding down to the ground and dancing around in juvenile humor. The boy tried to shield the undead's vision from the injured animal, causing the daemon to turn its head in odd directions, to continue to stare at the scene that had attracted its attention. This created more laughter from the group.

What on Nevidos are they doing? Realization hit him hard. *They're toying with it.*

Did they not understand just how dangerous that creature was? No, he suspected, they did not.

He could sense something, not an evil but a wrongness.

The boy in the back was now pantomiming the action of riding the sombra as he tried to bounce on top of the black mass of smoke and ephemeral power before falling through the creature or bouncing right off. A dark mass wriggled on the ground, unnoticed by the group of kids, squeezing up between the cracks of the stones. Like goo, but with bits jutting out.

What the hell—

The writhing mass shot past and through the boy that had been taunting it, and towards the boy who had the injured animal. The cries were fading, the creature's feet were no longer moving on the cobblestones, there was blood on the ground—Tsuske had not noticed that—had it just died? He noticed a makeshift spear, a branch that had been carved into a point, jutted out from the creature's abdomen.

"Look guys, look at it! It was so weak. Didn't stand a chance against me. What the—"

An arm—more like a tentacle—shot out from the mass of darkness, throwing the boy against the wall and reaching the small pink lifeless body on the ground. A purple shimmer surrounded the darkness. The thing bled vapor, a darkness that hissed and seemed to dissipate. No, not dissipating, but seeping inside the small body on the ground.

There was a shout from the kids as another tentacle shot towards them, wrapping around the legs of the one who had held the dying animal. The boy had tried to crawl away before he was hoisted into the air. It's head, what he thought was a head turned and regarded the boy, red eyes glowing, serrated teeth that formed from a slit mouth smiled up at the screaming boy before throwing him. The boy landed in a heap on the ground, unmoving. Silent.

Then, in a flash of darkness, the mass vanished into the dead animal, little tendrils wiggling at the mouth of the body before disappearing inside. Immediately, life flared up in the corpse, a dark energy radiating around it. Limbs jerking and bending with reanimation.

Tsuske rushed the entity while it was still taking host of its new body. Darkness seeped up from the ground in black and purple swirls, surrounding the crying youth. On the ground, shapes split from the swirling colors, becoming figures, as if their arms were pulling them up from a deep void.

They move like smoke, Tsuske thought.

"What are you brats still doing here, run!" Tsuske shouted.

The midnight creatures stepped away from the darkness as if from the surf. Legs sluggish, their bodies hunching. Their eyes searching. Of them all, one stood out as the biggest. Of all the darkness, the larger shape stepped forward—red eyes on him.

The mouth opened, sprouting spiny teeth.

"What the hell are you still doing here? I said run!" One of the shadow fiends turned towards the youth—towards the fallen boy who had not gotten up. Briefly, Tsuske wondered if he had been killed.

"Take your friend and get the hell out of here!" He saw that one kid, perhaps the one who had been standing by the entire time watching his friends, snapped up at the command and he scrambled to his unresponsive friend. Together, with the girl who could not stop crying, they pulled the unconscious boy down the street. There was no sign of the other kid who had been jumping on the creature just a minute ago. Tsuske hoped he had fled.

Standing in front of the mass of undead, he held forth the cage, cloth removed and with a dead animal laying inside. "Look at what I got here, look here!" he called out to the fiends. "Come and get it."

The creatures had two feet, and a body with arms and soon a head, that almost resembled that of a human. Except the creatures were almost translucent, the outer edges shiny with a dim purple light, with the inner body a deep darkness that he could almost see through; their features were blobby, imperfect. Not human.

He stood there, mesmerized by the line of forming monsters. Tsuske watched as they moved towards him, feeling a numbing trance settle over him. "I... know you," he whispered to the blackness, realizing how crazy that sounded and how true it felt.

The largest of the shadows stopped in front of the reanimated piglet. It was not as small as he had initially thought it to be. The size of a medium-sized dog. Blackness oozed out from around its snout, like shiny tar. Its eyes glowing a menacing red. Reaching down, it picked up the boar, each finger the length of its shadowy arms, moving like a grotesque tentacle around the wiggling undead animal. Then, with the mouth that was a slit, rows of needle-sharp teeth smiling at Tsuske, it swallowed its brethren.

The pig squealed and squirmed, its angry red eyes staring as its legs fought against the serrated teeth before vanishing down into the void. More beasts were showing up. The newer figures forming were distorted, more bestial as their arms touched the ground for support, spiny teeth spilling from their mouths, and tentacles forming on their backs.

He swung the metal cage backwards as he faced towards the enemy.

"You try to imitate us," Tsuske said in a whisper. "But you fail. They say you're just spirits. Lost and confused. Yet I can never forgive the monstrosity that you are. You killed my mother. My entire family deemed traitors because of you spirits. For that, you will die tonight, and you will stay dead!"

He pulled out his gun, releasing a dozen rounds into the swirling mass of smoke, the slugs bouncing off the side of the building. The things bled vapor, hissing smoke that then dissipated into the air.

All except for the one who had consumed the boar. The midnight face bristled with teeth as it smiled at him. With a raised outstretched arm, it pointed a finger at him.

An anger, a fiery fury, bubbled up inside of him. With a

quickness known by the COBRA, he pocketed his gun and pulled up the dagger and charged. Wisps of smoke emanated from the dark being, but Tsuske charged it. Dagger raised, he sliced down through the arm of the monster, splitting the arm in half. White bones falling to the ground with a clink, like the sound of steel boots striking the ground.

The sound echoed down the empty street. Two cloaked figures appearing at the opening where the youth had fled. A quick glance showed Tsuske that it was Nileen and Dmytro. They had come just in time. And then tendrils of darkness wrapped around him and he felt himself being lifted into the air, a cackling sound emanating from the creature's red eyes, mouth opening wide revealing rows upon rows of teeth, moving and writhing in a sucking motion. And then he felt the darkness holding onto him, let go. He fell down towards the teeth and the gaping mouth rushing up to meet him.

8

TSUSKE

Tsuske fell, sharp teeth, row after row, layer upon layer of spiny bone, rushed up at him as the shadow tendril—a tentacle—let go of him. He might have screamed, he might have fallen with honor to meet his death, but what he cannot remember was how the cage came into his hands just then.

With a crunch, the cage met the maw of the daemon and Tsuske hit the daemon and fell off of its body, falling and hitting the ground. He rolled to lessen the impact and to move away from the searching smoky strands of darkness. He could feel a cool breeze ensuing from the movements of the foreboding darkness.

"Tsuske, get up, run! We can take it from here!" It was Nileen's voice. He ignored her, pushing himself to his feet, stepping up to the darkness. In front of him, at the closest point near the shadows form, lay a white bony hand. Tsuske jumped forward, reaching for the bones, as the shadowy figure threw the cage away, as menacing eyes searched for him. A tentacle once writhe and wiggly, formed into a long dark spear as it shot right for him.

"Tsuske!" he heard gunfire and felt a tentacle around his leg, dropping him to all fours and throwing him against the wall. He flung himself away just as the tar-like spear slammed in where he had just laid.

"You should not have come," Tsuske panted as he stepped back towards his comrades. "We can't fight this. This is out of our capability."

"It's attracted to the dead animal. We still have ours and can lure it back towards the tower."

"No," Tsuske said, determined. "This one is different."

He watched as the mass of darkness, reflecting the light, like glistening tar with a purple soft haze of power that glowed around it, turned and slowly regarded them. With legs branching out below it, it hovered in the air. Like a wraith…

A wraith. A WRAITH?!

"Is that a wraith?" Nileen breathed.

"I have only heard legends of these things." Dmytro said, softly. "I had not thought them true."

"We can't fight this. We have to retreat." Tsuske backed away, his eyes never leaving the floating daemon.

"And leave the city to face its wrath?" Nileen turned to him. Her eyes wide. Tsuske could sense a protectiveness from within her that he had not thought possible. She was determined to see that this thing would harm no one. She wanted to keep the city safe. Dmytro at her side.

Am I the only sane one?

Behind him, he heard a hiss. They turned and met

darkness. On the ground, shapes split from the mass of black smoke, becoming figures. Sombra. He heard more than saw that Nileen and Dmytro both pulled forth their daggers. Suddenly the enemy moved with a burst of speed. He heard Dmytro cry out, and Nileen cursed, deflecting the reaching, clawing tentacles of darkness as the mass of swarming bodies swept up to them, and even along the sides of the walls. They surrounded them.

Tsuske was cut off from his team as the roiling forms of smoke and undead bodies surrounded him. Some creatures had hands, other had tentacles or spiny limbs growing where arms ought to have been. He cut and sliced with his dagger, smoke vaporing where his weapon went through. Faces were all around him, blobby features, imperfect smiles and eyes slitted or too round.

"Make for retreat," he hollered, hoping that they could hear him. "Fall back, fall back!"

The midnight figures dashed forward, charging him but he noticed that most flew around him—to his teammates. An explosion of frantic energy followed. Tsuske cut and swiped and even drew his gun and shot at the heads of roiling darkness. The bullets flew through them each and every time, the heads and bodies bursting into smoke before tar like appendages grew the slices, the holes, back together, noisily like cold water on hot stone; the creatures hissed. No longer were they the groaning, the moaning and tear-jerking cry of the undead, this was a horde full of menace and hatred and it sounded like a pit full of angry vipers.

Careful not to hit my comrades, the furtive thought flashed through his mind.

Something Nileen had said struck his thoughts. The way the undead moved around him like a boulder in the middle of a river, only a few of them fought against him. The rest sought his teammates. The two people who still carried dead animals in cages that were strapped to their backs.

"Give them the cages!" he shouted into the night. "Throw the cages! Make for retreat!"

He had not been sure that they had heard him. As he sliced through the formation of dark bodies as they tried to get at his team, he heard gunshots and hoped that none would strike at him. The darkness seemed to wade at the right flank, figures moving around him, and then suddenly ran in the opposite direction, scurrying like ants caught out in rain—or spiders rushing their prey. He finally saw his team. Both Nileen and Dmytro were pulling away from the bodies that had blocked them in, their weapons no longer piercing through the smoke, but sliding away, bouncing off.

"We have to get out of here," Tsuske said, sheathing his weapon and grabbing for Nileen and Dmytro's arms.

He turned, about to head down the street when he saw the darkness floating above them. Tendrils of smoke—tentacles—wiggled beneath the evil mass. Red eyes regarded them silently. Tsuske looked into the depths of the swirling void, the dark spinning soul of the wraith. And then the smoke dissipated, the sounds of angry hissing died away. He looked back the way the sombra had run to get to the cages and saw the street. A light mist had fallen, but it was dissolving. Street lights, colorful and vibrant, shined on the empty pavement. Merriment in the distance, the world was still in full celebration, unaware of the death that was plaguing the city. Unaware of all the commotion that he and his team had just experienced. He met the wide eyes of his comrades and turned back to the wraith. And to their surprise, it too, had vanished.

9

TSUSKE

"We will be executed," Dmytro said, simply. Emotionless.

The hallway seemed bleaker than normal in the ambient light that the torches provided. His comrade stirred, scrutinizing him. She wore an expression of control, but defiance etched at the corner of her mouth, and there was a spark in her bronze eyes that Tsuske had always admired. She saw him looking at him and the spark only grew.

"We're not going to die." She crossed her arms, leaning back against the wall, awaiting entry to the judgement room.

We're all going to die, Tsuske thoughts reflected Dmytro's words. The question is, whether it was today or tomorrow. Oh light. He hoped it would be today... didn't he?

He stared balefully at the Judgement Room doors and the two guards who waited outside. They had returned from their assignment as failures. And that could only mean one thing... death.

"What is with that look on your face, Tsuske?" Nileen demanded.

Tsuske glanced up at her. "We're all going to die one day. Today or tomorrow. We should not fret over the when or the how. It is just inevitable. Like everything else, we have to accept it."

"Do you hear yourself right now?" The storm in those eyes churning to life. If she were a thunderhead, Tsuske would be the lightning pull. "Are you just going to give up? Are you just going to toss it all in and say fuck it? Is your life really that meaningless? Because mine is not. I want to live, Tsuske. Live, you know, go out there, see the world, do things. Live."

"Live? Those things you mention are for those who have lives. We, our lives, are not our own, Nileen. You know this when you became COBRA. You chose this life. Live for the emperor or die a traitor's death. Die like the rest of our families did."

"And I shall live, committing myself to his whims, until my dying breath. I am no traitor. I chose this life for my family, to prove to them in their deaths that my family had honor in this life. I will serve the lord emperor until my death abdicates me of such a duty. But that doesn't mean we need to place our heads on the chopping block, does it? Do you want to submit like a cowed dog, meek with your tail between your legs, Tsuske?"

"Nileen," Dmytro nudged her gently. "Knock it off. Can't you see you're not helping the situation."

"Not helping? And what are you doing about it, you big oaf? Just standing around like a prized thoroughbred about to be sent to the slaughter because you didn't win the race!"

"Look, all I'm saying is maybe we need to come up with something." He looked uneasy, letting his feelings show. "I don't want to die. I also want to live." He stared at Tsuske.

"Look," Tsuske sighed. "We can't expect favoritism just because we are part of Director Voren's squad. We're replaceable. COBRA do not live long lives, and there is a reason for that. The lord emperor commands absolute loyalty accompanied by complete competence. Tonight, what we saw, what we failed in... he won't understand. We can't go in there believing that he will go easy on us. We have seen what he has done to squads of COBRA when they failed."

"Our numbers are so low, and yet, despite that, much is put on our shoulders," Nileen said in a whisper.

"Indeed," Tsuske said. "We're tasked with performing a luring and we did not bring back the undead that had been requested. We might have even caused more problems that we do not have answers for." He shook his head and paced. "We cannot fight those things. Those are not the sombra that the lord emperor and the scientists have ever seen before. Tonight, we failed in that mission. And quite possibly might have stirred the pot for rebellion."

"I know we failed in this mission. Failed in capturing the undead," Nileen said, looking confused. "What I don't know, is how our actions might have stirred anything up. Those daemons were already there. It's not our fault they're in the city. They're in droves down in the Grotto. Luring them away barely does anything for the amount that shows up. They just keep coming. Years ago, when I became COBRA, we might have done the luring's once a month. Now half the squads of COBRA perform luring's once or twice a week. And we still do not get them all. Sometimes they just get away. I don't see how this is any different."

"Tsuske, what do you mean by what you said?" Dmytro asked.

Tsuske caught a whiff of a sweaty, unwashed body and heard shuffling feet. He looked suspiciously to the side, expecting more guardsmen to show up—the tip to the iceberg that would prove their eminent death—but who came strolling forward was not who he had expected. A man, a massive man in gleaming black armor that seemed to radiate the firelight. The armor was seamless, no chains or bulky leathers, just smaller plates, incredibly intricate. The figure wore no helm, and his braided beard was nearly as long as his neatly tied back hair. At his waist was an ornamental sword, one no doubt that the man could wield if he needed too—the real weapons strapped to his back; large black fire power.

They were powerful. Sturdy. And beautiful. Like works of art. Tsuske had only ever seen some guardsman carry such powerful automatic weapons. They were reserved for the military. How could he have ever mistaken this warrior with that of regular footmen of the empire? General Gustaav of the imperial army strolled up to them. He had the face like most of the royal bloodline; angular, sharp and unkind eyes. First cousin to the lord emperor, Leon Leucii.

A position that Tsuske's family could have had in another life.

"Little Tsuske," the general said. "Good to see you're still alive. How's my favorite traitorous nephew doing?" The general laughed. "My brother's boy—you were always the shortest in the family. But then again... you are no longer part of the family, is that right?"

"Yes, General, sir." Tsuske's inside twisted and turned. He felt like he would be sick. This was his uncle, the brother to the lord emperor.

"Try not to embarrass yourself in there, today. You wouldn't want Director Voren to be shamed." The general moved towards the guards. "Announce me. The emperor is expecting me." A guard bowed respectfully and pulled the stone door open and went inside.

"Wait, General Gustaav." His uncle—no, no longer his uncle—turned to look at him, an eyebrow raised at the audacity he had to speak. "You said, Director Voren. How is he? He's in there?"

The door opened wide, the guard exited, holding the door open for the General. General Gustaav stared at Tsuske. A malicious smile tugged at the corner of his lips but he remained silent. Then he entered the judgement room, leaving Tsuske in the hallway with the other COBRA to ruminate on their failures and impending doom.

"THAT WAS THE GENERAL," Nileen said, her voice quivering. Tsuske looked at her and saw her eyes were wide as she bit at her lower lip.

General Gustaav was not a man who had risen to authority and power because he was the second-born brother of the lord emperor. He was well known in the military camps for his ruthlessness and cruelty.

"General Gustaav commands discipline and his soldiers are loyal to him," Dmytro said.

"Loyalty is the first lesson of a soldier's life, I would think." The first lesson to any person's life in the empire. Loyalty, duty and sacrifice. The people knew it well. "I would be worried if the guards and the soldiers had not mastered it."

Nileen sighed. "Must you always be so... so," her words drifted off.

"What?" Tsuske asked.

Nileen didn't reply.

"It's odd, how a leader, like General Gustaav, could affect his men," Dmytro said. "So many of these smaller versions of himself, seen in his soldiers. I'm surprised he hasn't tried to wrestle the power from his brother, the lord emperor."

"That is true," Nileen said. "They despise us. And everyone."

"But they're loyal to the general and the general is completely, without a doubt, loyal to the lord emperor and our ruler trusts that." Tsuske straightened his tie. "But that does not mean they are not to be watched. I would not trust them completely. The lower classes are mixed in the rabble." One-hundred to one. Those with imperial blood lines are made into officers, always to be above the lowborn. "The common soldiers do not have any honor."

"It is also another reason why they keep us around." Nileen nodded at his words as she starred off at the stone doors and the two guards who were guarding it. "Why would they need to guard the door like that, why from us, if the general trusts us?"

Dmytro scratched his nose. "They guard it from everyone. Even the servants."

"The servants have access through the backdoors—little passageways so they're not always caught under foot." Nileen leaned back against the wall, almost looking bored as she stuffed something white into her mouth. Tsuske narrowed his eyes, but he didn't question what it had been.

"It is why we never see them," Dmytro said.

"Oh, we see them," Nileen said. "But we see everybody. Even the little secrets that some think they can hide. We see through the shadows."

"Not for long," Tsuske said, his thoughts a mess. "The shadow is rising, that is something we cannot see and what we do not have answers to."

They fell into silence.

"What are we going to tell the lord emperor?" Nileen asked.

"I don't know. That we saw the sombra behaving oddly. That we failed the mission—but we had tried to bring them back with us. There were just too many sombra."

"He will not like to be told that," Dmytro said. "He will want answers. Answers we do not have for him. Where did they come from, he will ask of us? Where did they go? Who or what was that large one?"

"We have the security footage of the entire event on camera," Tsuske provided. But even he knew that would not be enough. Not for the lord emperor. It only provided more questions. Fewer answers. Less solutions.

"That was a wraith, wasn't it?" Nileen said. "You had told us, that at the power plant, you had seen it there. Was that the same one?"

Tsuske shrugged. "I don't know. It looked like it. It might have been the one. But how am I to say? It also looked very much like a sombra, too."

"A mutated one." Nileen retorted. "Much larger and... scarier. It commanded those in the street. I saw it. You both saw it."

"I don't know what I saw," Tsuske said.

"All right, fine." Nileen crossed her arms and her countenance heated again. "But I still say it was a wraith. Doesn't it bother you, Tsuske, that the undead are changing?"

"Legends," Dmytro began, and then he quieted and shook his head.

"What?" Both Nileen and Tsuske said together and then shot each other a look.

"What was that?" Tsuske said.

"There are legends about a wraith. A daemon lord. A shadow king. They're all the same but the stories speak of the wraith. It controlled the mindless spirits. Funny, the book is called The Shadow Rising, it is as if we are watching events unfold again."

"Why, Dim Dim, do you think that is funny?" Nileen said.

"The Shadow Rising?" Tsuske shot Nileen a look, hoping it would quiet her.

Dmytro hesitated, unsure who to answer first. "The Shadow Rising, an old book. It was in Doctor Axel's office. He had taken it with him to Bedeian, and I have not seen it for years. I do not know if it still exists. It is something we can mention to the Lord Emperor."

They waited and then Tsuske said, "all right, so what was so funny?" Nileen shot him a smug look, and he ignored it.

"Funny? Oh, yes, well, you had mentioned it. It got me into thinking about the book and where I had seen it." He looked over at him, his eyes full of curiosity. "Why had you mentioned it? Have you read that book?"

Tsuske opened his mouth to answer and then closed it. He had not been sure why he had mentioned it. It felt right when he had said it. But what had he meant by it? "I am not sure," he admitted. "Dmytro, you seem like you know what this book has written. What can you tell us about it?"

"Not much, I am afraid. I just remember seeing it in the good doctor's office. I had a glance at it, not more than a few pages read as I waited on the old man to be escorted."

"He just let you read what was on his desk?" Nileen asked.

"Well, no. He was distracted, and it bore me to wait," he said. Nileen quirked a smile at him.

"I probably would have done the same," she said. "Tsuske, do you have any of those old books from the witch's cot?"

The old books. He had completely forgotten about them, but something told him to err on the side of caution. "No, they must have been lost." Lost inside the duffle bag that he had carried with him to the power plant. Left behind at the foot of Director Voren's bed back in the hospital. He wondered if they had even survived the removal from the cottage—they had been so old.

"That's too bad," Nileen said, looking disappointed. "Something in them might have helped us. I remember something in them that had mentioned something about secrets. Do you remember it Tsuske?"

"No, I don't." He shook his head.

"You had been reading them out loud," she said. "Something about secrets."

"Sorry, I don't remember."

"Damn it," Nileen said.

"Don't worry, Nileen. It was only a little hope." He sighed and leaned back against the wall. "I remember reading about the Ancients in that old volume but did not know it at the time how important was the old book I had been reading. Something about the Ancients having the power to stop the sombra—to push them back. Shadow and the light. What is it that they could do that we cannot do now? Why did they do it? We don't know."

"We know enough," Nileen said. "They used elaborate

tricks to imitate great powers and pretend to be all holy. But when their deceptions were discovered, they fled."

"That is just what some monks say, I do not think it to be true," Tsuske said.

"Oh really, and you think they're wrong? They have all the history of the world in their temples. Why do you think the lord emperor holds them so close?"

"Why indeed?" Tsuske said.

Nileen paused and gave Tsuske a searching look. "You think something is there, don't you? Something that they are not telling us?"

"Perhaps," Tsuske said lightly. "Why is it that the lord emperor allows for only one religion without retribution? Why is the monkhood encouraged to do public speaking's? Why are the people given penalties for now showing?"

Nileen frowned. "Because it's the one true religion and that others should believe as they do?"

"It makes little sense," Tsuske said. "Something is there, something hidden. Knowledge, secrets, no doubt. But could whatever be there, aid us?"

"If we survive this evening, we will need to investigate," Nileen said.

"Look lively," Dmytro said quietly. "I think our doom awaits us."

The doors to the judgement chamber opened, stone grinding upon stone. Light flooded out into the dark ill-lit corridor and the two guards standing watch stepped aside.

"The Lord Emperor will you see you three," one of the guard's said.

"Guns, guts and glory," Nileen said as she gave Tsuske's

shoulder a firm squeeze and then took Dmytro's arm firmly into hers' for a quick squeeze. Tsuske had liked the feel of her hands on his arm, though he said nothing. He wondered if it would be the last touch from a close comrade he would receive before his head was on the chopping block.

10

TSUSKE

Dozens of faces turned to them as they entered the room. The guard's eyes roved over their bodies for the weapons they kept concealed. Sentries in black protective armor, not as ornate or fine as the generals, but protective leathers and fibers that gave them the right appearance as the general's loyal soldiers. Soldier's loyal to the lord emperor.

Tsuske stepped forward into the unusually cool, dim room, and with a deferential bow, arms in the correct salute, they bowed at the waste; Nileen performing the masculine form of respect. This did not seem to upset the lord emperor as he was used to this gesture of respect coming from the snakes. COBRA only had one correct way. The lord emperor twitched his fingers, and Tsuske and his team rose from their deference.

So dark... the room had never been so dark in all of his memory. *Nor so cold.*

The door slid open once more and the lord heir

accompanied by the chancellor came into the room; Tsuske knew that his entourage of guardsmen would be left in the hallway to await their departure.

"My son, what have you been getting up to?" the emperor's voice was a bitter, cold voice that held the assurance of obedience a hundred times over. A voice that disliked having a child who did not obey his commands. "I had asked for you to arrive earlier. If you were not my child —I would have sent your away."

"Father—" Tobias began, but the lord emperor cut him off.

"You have been down seeing that animal again, it seems, son." Tobias plucked a stray glossy black feather from his imperial regalia, and then promptly stuck the feather behind his ear. "If fact," the emperor went on calmly, "it would seem that despite my orders to the contrary, you have contrived to take your time to be with that animal—"

"—That animal is supposed to be mine to bond. It's still a young chick. Bigger than the others, and nearly as tall as me! We just separated him from his mother—who would have thought that a pair of brood Mosaien were something to reckon with. The bird keepers assured me I had to be there throughout the process. Not during the process of luring and capturing the chick and sequestering it to its own aviary. I was required to be there when the chick was mewling: to provide it comfort." The heir raised his chin a little as he said the last part in defiance.

"I would have thought better of you, Tobias. You must learn to obey. Use your head of yours; counterweight them against your actions. This meeting takes precedence over taming a war animal." The emperor's eyes flashed green as they settled on his son. "I'll be assigning you permanent COBRA to escort you to and from appointments from now on. I'll be giving them the authority to make you obey me. Do not shame yourself by trying to argue."

"But father—"

"Learning to obey, learning to become the next emperor. That is as much the duty of the lord heir as it is to ride war animals and learning to wield a gun or sword. Perhaps if your training is intensified, you will find less time for dalliances. I will ask Director Voren for a couple of his COBRA to become your permanent retainers."

Tsuske observed the general looking uncomfortable at this, his mouth moving like he wanted to speak, instead his lips narrowed to a thin line as he held his silence.

Tobias shifted his feet as if about to protest, then bowed his head instead. "As you command, father." There was a defiant look in his eyes. Tsuske wondered if the lord heir would voice his discontent.

"My lord," General Gustaav's eyes swung to Tsuske, then quickly looked away. "I think I can assign some chaperones for the boy."

"I think I have spoken, general," the Lord Emperor said.

"I don't think the snakes have enough people to provide both the spy network when the lord heir is on route and be his personal escort."

"Oh, you don't think so?" The lord emperor's head turned to regard someone Tsuske did not see. "What say you on this matter, Voren?" Voren? Tsuske's head turned. Was he here?

"We should be able to muster it, just fine." The voice was quiet, too soft for the director's. Could that be him?

"See?" The lord emperor turned back to the general who stood beside him. "Looks like they can carry that assignment out just fine."

"We'll see," the general said.

"Father," Tobias protested, "I mean to obey you. Truly, I do."

"You do?" The lord emperor asked in mock surprise, then he shook his head. "You constantly test how far you may go. I did the same to my father. I think all four of us did until our oldest brother died. Then that spirit was refined when my father named me the heir. You have disobeyed me and have had taken your time to bond with the weaned chick. Be satisfied that I have decided to spare its life and not make it for tonight's feast. My will still stands. You will have a COBRA chaperone on top of your ordinary guard protection."

Tobias bowed his head sullenly. The will of defiance still strong in his eyes.

"Director Voren, there is a matter at hand. I would like your input on." The Lord emperor's gaze fell onto Tsuske. "What do we do with traitors?"

"FLAY THEM. String them up. Hang them. Decapitate them. We have a lot of methods of punishment that fit the crime."

"That is quite the list," the emperor said.

Why are his eyes lingering on me? I have committed no

such an act. His mind reeled and briefly he recalled words he had spoken earlier. Words he had regretted. Wrong words spoken are crimes against the empire. Traitors words. No! I was on assignment.

"Tsuske, step forward," the general said, a cruel smile on his face. "You are here today, for a crime against the empire. An allegation that is being said that you have spoken words of lies and betrayal—if proven true, you will stand before the lord emperor as a traitor. Do you understand?"

"What?" He heard Nileen demand behind him. "He would never do such a thing. How dare you declare him a traitor or even being of that ilk. He is loyal—the most loyal man I have ever met!" Her words shocked him to his bones and made his heart swoon. She had been a loyal comrade for the five years he had worked alongside her.

"I would like it repeated, what Tsuske has said that is being considered." Director Voren's voice of reason spoke above the gloom that was settling over him, and he clung to it. It was not as strong as he was used to hearing it. He looked around the room and spotted the older man in a small chair attached to wheels at the back of the room. Their eyes met for a brief moment and his heart nearly fell to his feet. Director Voren looked pale, aged and ill. His eyes fell to the stump of a leg and the missing arm. Why was he not still in the recovery room?

"Certainly," a voice said, one that Tsuske had heard never heard before. "You see, I overheard him and derive his plan this past evening. Unlike the general's ideas of his being a traitor, I do not believe it. You see, I think he was acting."

Tsuske's mind reeled. *When had this man...the chancellor been around?*

"Acting?" The lord emperor's eyes narrowed.

"It is part of the job," Director Voren said bluntly. "Sometimes we have to play a part to gather intelligence."

"Lies," General Gustaav said. "I have a guard that had overheard him this evening. When I heard the Chancellor speak that he heard a snake speak words of a traitor, I had inquired in with one of my guard that had been put on duty and so happened to be patrolling the area. He had heard it too and believe it to be the truth. A ploy to rile rebellion."

Rebellion?

Director Voren laughed. It was weak, hollow, but he laughed. They had dimmed the lights except for those that surrounded Tsuske and his team—even the stone fireplaces held no light and none of their usual fires.

"You find something humorous in treason?" The general asked.

"None at all. You are a complete fool, general."

"When did you say you overheard the boy speak these things, chancellor?" Director Voren looked at the odd man that stood near the Lord Heir.

"Today, not long ago, in fact. I was the barkeep. Surely Tsuske recognized me."

Tsuske stared in alarm. *How much had he heard?*

"Voren, you vouch for this boy, that he be not a traitor?" The emperor's voice commanded honesty.

"My lord emperor, he is as loyal and true, as I am."

"My youngest brother's ilk." The lord emperor glanced at

Tsuske. Then leisurely raised a vial to his mouth and took a sip. "I trust you, Voren—my only friend. Trust you more than I do the brothers I have killed. You were always loyal to me."

"Very," Director Voren said without an ounce of amplification. "Sweet, Sweet pillows friends."

The lord emperor laughed, a loud, throaty sound that echoed throughout the room. "Careful, Voren, you would not wish to make my only living brother jealous."

General Gustaav turned away, shaking his head in disgust. "My lord emperor, please."

"Well, you vouch for this boy, then I will take your word on it." The emperor took his eyes off the general and turned to the director. "How are you feeling out of bed so soon after surgery?"

"Tired," the director's voice said quietly. "If we can get this adjourned, I believe I had better rest. If Doctor Axel finds me here, he'll never leave me alone."

"A completely prosthetic arm and leg will look good on you."

"By tomorrow morning, I will be a new man," the director slurred. "And tomorrow morning I'll deal with Tsuske on a more personal hand. What is important is that the people know we have a plan? That they see us acting on this issue that we are being presented with. We need to be seen as the light that is conquering this darkness that the people so rightfully fear. And that they see you are party of that victory, Leon."

The lord emperor grunted and then turned to Tsuske. "What exactly was it you said? The video feed has been shown and I have the head scientist reviewing the tapes as we speak."

Tsuske took a deep breath and retold what had happened; starting from the beginning when the mission had begun and his meeting with Quetzal and then the sombra and the wraith appearing. The room fell into silence as his words trailed off at the end. A wraith and it had disappeared into the night, leaving the three of them in the streets. Then there was one more thing he remembered. A lump in his pocket spoke of its secrecy.

"There is one other thing," he said, pulling his hand from the cloak. Tsuske opened his hand and looked down at the long white finger bones—thrice the size of a normal man's hands. He had forgotten about these. "These belong to the wraith."

A low crack rang in the air as Director Voren fell out of the chair, and hit the ground, like someone dropped a bag of bricks. Tsuske's head snapped around, looking to where the director had sat and seeing him on the ground. His stumps were bleeding again.

He ran forward, but a woman beat him to him. Another COBRA, one who had stood hidden in the shadows. His memory raced for a name, Mayori. "My lord, he needs to be seen by a doctor or a group of healers. His wounds have reopened."

"Go, get him back to the hospital. Have them install his prosthetics tonight. Tell them I command it on pain of death for failure or his death. See that it is done."

"Yes, my lord!" Carefully, she got him back onto the chair and slowly carted him away. As the unconscious

Voren passed him, he saw that the director was not completely knocked out. And as he was pushed away, he thought he saw the director wink at him. The door had been opened and then closed behind them.

"Now then, what was that you showed me?"

Tsuske opened his hand again, revealing the long white bones of a severed hand, lacking muscle and sinew, only the glistening white bones.

The lord emperor studied what was in his hand, not so much as beckoning him forward for a closer look. Then, more grimly with an edge to his voice he said, "Go, fetch Nakamatsu. Immediately."

The general signed to two of the guards to leave their post and carry out the task. Then his eyes fell to Tsuske too. Weighing and judging him and what he had brought forward this evening. Then he nodded, never taking his eyes from his face. Tsuske met his gaze with a levelness that belied the sour feeling in his gut. He noted the steadiness of his look and judged that he had made a personal enemy of the general this evening.

11

TSUSKE

"This is interesting," Professor Yoshi Nakamatsu said. "Where did you get it?" The man had walked in without preamble and did not seem concerned with the impertinence of the soldiers who had held their swords to the scientist to hasten his speed. Despite the threat, he seemed to walk as the one in control. Tsuske saw the soldiers sheathe their swords as they entered and took their places of watch once more.

Really? he thought, *did they need to draw arms on the scientist?* He had not thought it to of worked. He had never seen the scientist run before and did not expect to.

"A wraith," the scientist said, thoughtfully. "I will need to study this, my lord emperor."

"A wraith?" The emperor's voice grew dark. "Did you not promise me we had this under control?"

Professor Yoshi Nakamatsu's mouth tightened into a line. "That situation is under control, my lord. This—this is something new. I will need to study it. To understand it and give you proper answers."

"Fine, do as you must. You have always provided answers when I have needed them."

Professor Yoshi Nakamatsu put a waxy white glove over his hand as Tsuske handed over the bones. "Tell me, boy, did it just let you go?"

Tsuske shrugged. "We didn't flinch when it attacked us."

Professor Yoshi Nakamatsu nodded thoughtfully. "Interesting. Your team has done well."

"Well enough that I can look over their failure this time," The lord emperor said. "Next time may be different. We need to lure the daemons here so you can study it. Nakamatsu, how is it that you can contain the creatures?"

"Carefully with containment wards. They're like what keeps the Gestahl afloat, but more refined."

"A barrier?" Tsuske asked.

"They're all over—few know of their existence. It is why the capital city has been sombra free for so long." The scientist pocketed the bones into his clean, white lab coat. "It would be a nuisance if people knew about the wards. Keep it to yourself."

"Do other COBRA know of it? Does the director?"

"He knows," the general said. "All the elite do." And now, so did many of General Gustaav's soldiers in the room. Could they be trusted?

"I see," Tsuske said. Nileen at his side nodded, folding her arms. Dmytro looked thoughtful and then nodded as if it all made sense. Containment wards. *Why was this not common knowledge for the COBRA?* Why was he just now finding out about them?

It's as if they do not trust us or maybe it's me they do not trust. A paranoid way to think, perhaps, but this was his job. To keep the empire safe. To do as the lord emperor commands. It made sense. They had lured sombra to the tower before, to be studied by the professor. Why had he never thought about it before?

"The entire city has this warding, then?" Tsuske asked. "Why is it we do not feel it when flying out of the city on helibird or sky-trams?"

"They are begemmed with the counter ward. Those without wards would be hit with what would feel like glass."

Tsuske couldnt help but wonder why then were birds and rain able to pass through the wards. *What made them different?* He had no time or authority to be voicing his concerns at this moment. These were answers that he would have to find out on his own.

That didnt stop other snakes from asking questions. "I don't understand why we are only finding out about this now?" Nileen said. "We are COBRA. It is our duty to know everything in order to do our jobs."

"You would have understood if you had taken the time to think about it," the general said. "COBRA and my soldiers lure the sombra to the palace occasionally. Where do you think they go?"

"He is right," Tsuske said. "It makes sense."

They locked gazes. He pressed his will into her's. *Back down, Nileen. This is not the time or place to pick a fight. Not here. Not now. We have just narrowly escaped with our heads still on our shoulders.* As if sensing his thoughts, she deferred and looked down at her feet.

She didn't look happy. "Yes, it makes sense now that you say so."

"You will need to get back out there and find this creature again."

"What?" Tsuske asked sharply. He looked up sharply. It was not the lord emperor that had spoken, but the scientist. Surely, he had misheard.

"You need to find it and bring it here. It is the only way we can study it," then as if an afterthought he said, "and protect the people and the empire at the same time."

"My lord emperor," Tsuske pleaded. "We are not capable of fighting this thing. We do not have the power. Maybe if we had a ward to protect ourselves, or to enclose it off. But we do not have that power, my lord. It will be dangerous."

"Are you so afraid of danger, Tsuske?" The emperor asked. "Do this for me and you will rise in my books. Fail— and face the consequences of being inconsequential. I will make use of the COBRA one way or another. I have need of competent, loyal men."

"Remember the sermons that the monks speak," the general said. "Remember your duty."

"My lord—use us as you have always used us. This is not who we are. We cannot do this. Not how we are now."

"Do it, son of my youngest brother, and bestow honor back onto your side of the family. Where they rest, give them honor and pride in their deaths, or must you disgrace them with your failures?"

Tsuske swallowed and looked down.

"They are COBRA, but they still have their dreams and dignity, father," The lord heir said in a whisper, a whisper that had been meant to carry. "They are COBRA so it is their right to make sure the empire is safe, and they may die doing their duty. But their honor is always their own. You cannot give or take it from them."

The lord emperor grunted. "You have been around too many non-believers of late. You will need to listen to the monks when they speak, son, less you fall into disgrace and dishonor. You would not make for a good COBRA."

The monks, a voice whispered in his mind. A woman's voice. *They had been Higaziit at one time. Branching out throughout the world, traveling with the children of the dawn. Then as time passed, they became influenced by greed and selfishness. They changed. The ardents of the monastery of One Life had changed. Their purpose had changed.*

Tsuske felt his brow furrow as he thought.

Improve thyself by sacrifice. Better thyself by your obligations to the empire and the higher powers. Dream small, for the collaboration of all dreams makes for a big dream under the empire. Unity. Prosperity. Humble thyself. Walk in the shadow of the one true lord as the empire is the vestige of the higher powers. See unto it and see the glory of the gods and goddesses and the gift they bestow upon the believer.

Its all wrong, the voice mourned. *That is not the way.*

It has always been the way, he thought to the voice.

Only the elite could dream big. He had been part of that family long ago. Why shouldn't men like him be expected to dream big dreams? If he had fallen as the countless other before him, why could others not dream? None of it seemed to fit. Society and religion, they contradicted each other. Why would one walk of life have a more impact on the gift that the gods given?

Perhaps you can think for yourself...

Wait! Who are you? he asked the voice.

The voice contradicted what he had been taught but was it wrong?

Soldiers and those who were seen to sacrifice themselves were glorified within the empire. Seen as above others. Yet—without smithies, miners, craftsmen and farmers, a soldier was little more than a man without armor. A man without clothes. A man with hunger. Being different was not sacrilegious—or those who were glorified would not be what their fate had led them to become.

Better yourself with a calling in life that will better others. Don't get too ambitious or we'll brand your family a traitor and lock you away in servitude as a snake.

Only you can unlock the truth to the lies you yourself believe...

Who are you?!

He shook his head to dispel the voice and his thoughts. "Where would you have us go?" he asked.

The scientist stared at him, a curious look on his face. "I would advise the mines down in the grotto before anywhere else."

"Why the mines?" The lord emperor asked. "Why not the streets of Gestahl? Forget about the Grotto, the people up here are the ones that matter."

"Of course, my lord," Professor Yoshi Nakamatsu said. "but the daemons are not up here to kill us."

"Then why are they suddenly up here?" This came from the general. "I say we tighten security and send all the snakes after this thing. If they all die but bring back the thing with one of them alive, that would be enough."

"Tighten security is obvious," Professor Yoshi Nakamatsu said with a wave of his hand, dismissing it. "But the sombra are not here for us. They want what we have."

"What is it we have?" The lord emperor asked, narrowing his eyes.

"What we have always had. Power."

"The sombra want our power?"

"Why else are they always where they ought not to be? It attracts them as much as they are attracted to death and those dying."

"The power plants? The vessels that support Gestahl's levitation?"

"Those are good places to tighten security around and lure away any unwanted visitors."

"Then where?" The emperor demanded.

"The mines," the professor said tersely.

"The mines?" the general folded his arms, heavy armor creaking with the movement. "They have been practically useless for months. Too many of the things keep popping up there. Peasants are too cowardly to work in them."

"Something is there that attracts them. We need to find out what it is. If something is there, we need to seize it before we can capture this wraith."

"Very well," the lord emperor said. "Tsuske, you and

your team of snakes will go to this mine and find out what is there. Be covert—don't let on to the other COBRA of your mission. If there is something there, try to take it from the daemons, wrestle it from their fingers if you have to. And bring back that wraith alive, sacrifice someone to lure it if you must. I command that you do this. If you fail me again..." his words trailed off on the threat.

Tsuske could only nod and then bow. They had been given another chance at escaping death. Without Director Voren's influence and support, they were surely doomed. Death, something he had longed for would come when they failed this mission. With certainty, he knew that there would be zero chance of success. From the looks from those in the room and that of his comrades, they knew it too.

12

TSUSKE

They exited the aerial tramway station after it touched down on the sodden wet ground of the lower cities. His foot smooshed into wet foliage, leaves having been left over and forgotten about after the upper city had celebrated the autumnal festival a few months back. He glanced skyward. Dimly he could see the outline of the circular mass floating a mile above them. Past it, the roiling clouds let down their downpour of hoarded water.

How I have been such a fool, he thought as he stared. How had I never noticed that there was a barrier around the city until now? It had been dry up in the capital. The street pristine and clean, the air still and pleasant for the New Year's festivities. But sometimes, the streets were awash in rain and winds. *Who was in charge of the barrier and what were the deciding factors or shutting it off?*

"I guess they can shut it off when they want to," Nileen said. He glanced over at her, seeing she was staring up at what he was looking at: the city high above.

My thoughts are becoming too visible for the others to see. I need to get myself together...

Dmytro stood near Nileen and he too looked up at the city as if this was the first time he had seen it from down below. "A city will collect dust if there is no wind and rain. Easier and probably cheaper to allow the natural elements to cleanse things than to hire Grottons to do the work. Though cheap labor that most Grottons may be. Free is even better."

"Come on, it isn't far from here," Tsuske said, turning away from the monolith.

The people at ground level gathered in the shadow of Gestahl; all thirteen cities of the Grotto. Cities that represented the western countries and the kingdoms that had once stood large, tall and proud long ago when they had come together, in unity. Civilizations that had governed themselves. During a time when the eastern empire had unified and had welcomed the western world into peace and unity. Thirteen cities had been born. Building below the hovering capital city of Gestahl. At one time, the stories said that Gestahl did not fly but had stone legs that connected it to the ground and a massive staircase leading up to its pearly gates where the elite of all the world's people gathered for amalgamation.

That had been a millennium ago, long, long before the eastern empire, the Gestahlian empire as it is known now, unified the western countries. For several hundred years now, the western countries have lived under the rule and influence of the east. The thirteen cities of Grotto living beneath the capital city. Providing sucker, life support and the means for the wealthy to continue to live a life of greed.

Thirteen cities all cobbled together in a semblance of civilization beneath the almighty power of the empire. It was not a spotless mirage of the cities and the kingdoms that had been their former glory. Structures to live in were made up of scrap metal and rubble and further away from the central mass of buildings, the worse for wear the people's lives became. From the scraps of what once had been, came the ideals and the culture of the people of the Grotto. No one recognized themselves as anything but Grotton.

Hierarchy formed in the means of district street lords, with those who would thrive and prosper at the top and everyone else just trying to find a means to survive. If they were lucky, they could find a job at a hiring center, usually ran by one of those district lords. With luck comes food for their families, clothes for their backs, and a ramshackle shelter.

Then there were those who had been unlucky, either died on the street of the Grotto or found themselves in a cell awaiting the administrations of a madman to test out his next set of theories. It did not matter if the people were innocent of crimes and had lost their job because of illness or were ruthless murderers out looking for their next victim. If they did not check in at the hiring center and pay their taxes, with proper documents completed, a pair of soldiers would eventually find them and escort them to a place where they would be useful.

Despite it all—the people of the Grotto worshipped the

empire and the divine monks who brought them the peace and unity their forefathers had fought so hard against. The people saw the virtue of a powerful ruler governing over them, protecting them against the unseen enemy in the night. Was it not true that the rebellious scum in the west had hordes of the undead at their doorsteps? Was it the sins of their people that had brought it upon themselves? No, the west was on their own, they would get no sympathy from those of the Grotto or topside in Gestahl.

The ardents had told of the coming of gods and their gifts of divinity, and how the empire would be at the top of them all. To prove their faith in the gods, to prove loyalty and undying servitude, they supported the empire and in doing so; they served them. There would always be a faction that would rise, speaking bouts of rebellion, a traitorous word to the nonbeliever. Those easily beguiled listened to them and join in their cause—which would end sourly for them when the snakes overhead their talks of treason.

"I hate it down here," Nileen said. "The people are nothing but slaves to the decadence of the top-side elite."

"Quiet, Nileen." Tsuske shot her a glare. "We narrowly escaped with our heads for one last chance. Let's not call this mission prematurely over and have the general's men called down upon us." Though he might welcome death. His heart felt a twang. Was it guilt? No, he did not welcome death, not if it meant that his comrades would face the same fate as he. He couldn't help but feel confused, conflicted and guilty for feeling these.

What is wrong with me?

Nileen scoffed. "As if these people would do such a thing. They see us and they run and hide. The things we say might be a ruse to lure them into a trap. It's how their minds work."

"We don't need the unwanted attention. We have a mission to complete."

"You and I both know that will not happen. This will not be successful, Tsuske."

"Won't you just do as I say for once?" He shot at her, heat in his voice. "You are always wanting to pick a fight and I won't be goaded into one. I am your leader while Director Voren is out."

"Me? It's you who act like you have something to prove. Your feelings are finally coming out." She shot right back at him. "Maybe that is because you act like you have a reason to die."

"Yeah—well... maybe I do," he said. He knew that he was seeking to cover up his shame—the shame of being the sole survivor of his family when his family had been killed for treason. Treason only he could be blamed for. *But why am I only just now thinking of this?* His thoughts were muddled, unfocus.

I need to focus.

"Tsuske, I know something in you is hurting, we all have experienced that pain. Myself. Dmytro. All the COBRA. But you can't go about wanting to kill yourself."

"I don't want to kill myself." *Lies...* these were blatant lies; lies he would need to continue to tell himself. "I have a duty to fulfill whether I believe it would be successful."

A firm hand gripped his arm. He turned, readying to

confront Nileen. When he turned the brown eyes of Dmytro met his. He was one to usually keep his peace and his thoughts to himself, much like Tsuske. Tsuske appreciated the silent comfort of one who was similar to himself.

"My sister had been killed for seeking medical treatment for a child down here in the mining district. I hate it down here. This place holds too many memories for when my family came down here to govern the shipping of crates top side. The tower found out, and the child was to be turned over to the science department for 'treatment'. My sister refused, and the one in charge brought soldiers to our manor and executed her in the courtyard. All of my neighbors saw. My parents were away at the docks, securing shipment so they did not know. I saw it from my bedroom window. I became the sole survivor of my parents' line after an explosion the same day killed them."

Tsuske was taken aback by the admission. He had not been made Second in command and kept out of the loop. He had learned about all the members of COBRA and how they had fallen into the role of the snake. He waited, allowing Dmytro the time to voice his thoughts as he was one to speak only rarely.

"As you may know, my family had also fallen out of line. It was a time when the harvest failed to bring in what was due. No one had ever figured out what had gone wrong and the mistakes have not been repeated, but ten years ago was a difficult time in history. There had been rebellion growing down here and my parents were supposed to see to it. Harvest had come in, and they ignored the issue at hand and focused on the supply lines. Supply lines that carried fresh foods and goods. Some street gangs had caused the populace to grow agitated with their debauchery. They stole from the people and the empire had to pay the price. The angry citizens were only hungry and trying to feed their families. They attacked the shipping docks while my parents were there, and the emperor was forced to send in the military. Eventually the rabble died down and people forgot why they had been upset when food was suddenly right in front of them. The emperor had tactfully dished out some of those supplies to the people before securing the shipments, the boundaries, and reigning the people in. Despite the support, my parents had died by the explosion."

"That left you head of the house."

"I was underage. I could not be head of house. The empire decided to revoke my privilege of birth and bestow it onto another. Someone who had grown in favor and risen in influence and power. Probably whoever that had helped with the rebellion. And I? I learned to survive by crawling on my belly like a serpent for the mistakes of my parents."

They splashed toward the mines; the city streets of the Grotto seemed to be teaming with people despite the fat raindrops that fell. The Grottons ignored the three individuals in dark cloaks, hoods drawn to their faces. Grim faced, eyes at their feet, they seemed determined not to attract the attention of someone they did not know. The night was getting late, but despite the hour, there would be workers traveling together to and from work. The factories employed people at all hours of the day. Work did not halt because of the time of day or the hour of the night—production managers demanded that supplies to be produced because the high lords in the city above required it.

"Director Voren once told me something," Tsuske blurted, wondering why he was even speaking it aloud. It had been a private conversation between the man he admired and himself. "In order to do good, we sometimes have to be bad."

The other two remained quiet and he could feel their eyes on his back. They walked on in silence, allowing his thoughts to come up. His feelings. "I don't really understand it. Yet—it is something that our director lives by. He has thrown his life to duty and obligation. That is how he retains his honor. Despite being used and his body torn apart, he believes in those words. He believes that to do some good in this world, you have to do bad acts. Or be bad for the greater good. Even if you despised yourself.

I don't know if I can live by that. My parents died, believing in something similar. It was the Higaziit way. If you see the light, then it is your duty to show others the heavens beyond the clouds. Life of others before your own. Shoulder their worries so that others can see the light beyond the shade of their burdens. In my mind, it is the words of a servant. A man born of servitude. A slave.

This servitude, this sacrifice of your morals and of your honor, is seen as a virtue by our society. It is too much for me to bear, at times. Please forgive me for my weakness."

He had never spoken out loud about his problems

before and he couldn't help but feel the shame of his failures.

They passed a closed off area, the sounds of the city, the factories and the surrounding neighborhood seemed to fade as they walked into the abandoned area of the mines. Tall buildings around them sat dormant, dark and quiet. The pit lay just beyond the courtyard up ahead. A large slope that would lead them into the mines. Without workers, the pit's lanterns had not been lit. Only the courtyard and buildings were lit by lantern and lamp light. Up ahead appeared a pool of blackness. One wrong step would lead to a world of pain or death.

Tsuske turned the long leather strap over in his hands, adjusting the weight placed on his shoulders. It was almost a hand span wide and a finger thick. And it helped carry the wounded animal on his back. Feeling the guilt of having to carry the poor beastly thing in a cage during its last hours of life. It had been poisoned. A slow and excruciating death, all in the name of the greater good.

"Tsuske," Nileen said softly. "I don't know what to say. I…"

"Say nothing. There isn't anything that is needed to be said. I'm not looking for sympathy, instead, this I tell because I thought you both may need to know it. If we fail here, it isn't because we failed to try. It isn't because we lacked the equipment. We failed because I lack virtue and the lord emperor, my uncle, wishes to punish us because of me."

"That isn't true, Tsuske. The lord emperor wishes no

such thing. You are only confused. You have virtue, you're the most honorable man that I know. You—"

"I don't need to hear your platitudes, however true or false you believe them to be. I don't want to hear it."

"But—"

"Nileen, enough." Dmytro cut in. "Tsuske needs to work this out on his own. Give him time to think. This is something that he needs to learn and know on his own."

Tsuske felt a growl come up from his throat before he could stop it.

"Well, he is learning how to show how he feels," Nileen said. "A bit primal but he's learning."

He shook his head. The main entrance to the mine was up ahead. Soft moans, the cries of a wounded soul pierced through the night. The sounds of the dead could be heard in the wind as the rain splattered onto the ground all around them.

"Who's ready to die tonight?" he asked humorlessly.

"The hell to that!"

Facing towards the entrance of the pits, he shouted. "Guns, guts and glory!" and charged into the dark looming void ahead.

13

TSUSKE

Tsuske had not been assigned to this squad by chance. Out of all the COBRA, Director Voren's squad had known the most casualty in the years past. By some miracle, by the grace of the spirit of the ancients, his team had had no deaths in the past five years since he had been assigned to this squad. That was notable, considering that the average COBRA squad often lost one out of four of their number every year. The emperor had placed his brother's only child with the director, knowing the risks that the man liked to take.

Of the sixty-four men and women who were enlisted with COBRA, nearly twenty to thirty percent of that number would be killed in action every year. The surviving squads would be combined, trying to keep members together or fresh snake material added to their number, where they would eventually die. It did not matter the arrangement.

The fallen COBRA would be replaced. Replenished with

more unfortunates whose families have committed any number of perceived crimes against the empire, and then those too would die. Squad leaders after squad leaders being chosen. It was supposed to be a favored position on a squad, one earned from merit and competence. Tsuske wondered why he had been chosen.

Some missions weren't as bad. If they had a plan and the right equipment to establish control over the target, nobody died. And if they needed backup, another squad would be called in for assistance. If it became extreme, the military would be called in and the COBRA would withdraw. Their skills were better placed elsewhere than in an open combat. Even in a bad run, the target would rather flee with their life than to stay for a firefight and face the imperial army. And then there were those times when the target would rather attempt to blow up the oil fields or throw dynamite into the mines. Sometimes they would rather attempt to escape with the wagons or trains of supplies than to flee the scene. Domestic or foreign affairs —they were similar. Follow this, destroy that, protect this or assassinate that, capture them or make it disappear. Go here. Go there. Guard this. Kill that.

Dmytro and Nileen walked close behind, with Tsuske taking the lead. His lantern light attached to a short poll that stuck up from the cage on his back and up, over his head, illuminating the vast chamber of the mines and all the dark holes, the mine shafts, that branched out and beyond. These two had been part of Director Voren's team a year longer than he had been. He'd replaced a fallen comrade when his family had been disgraced and dispatched. His family all gone. The Higaziit were no more. All except for him.

He should have done something. The disgrace had been imminent. And he should have done something. His father had been the lord emperor's third brother. The youngest of the triplets born to the previous emperor, who also sired several older now deceased children. His father had defied his father's wishes, the previous emperor, and had married a Higaziit instead of one of the high lords of Gestahl. His father had married a Higaziit, reestablishing the family bloodline with the old bloods of the west. His father had seen it as a means for peace. A means of unity such as the empire proclaimed. But the Higaziit were known traitors of the empire, and the marriage had been seen as sacrilege. Creating feuds and anger amongst the high lords and great houses of Gestahl.

Of the thirteen kingdoms to the west, the Higaziit were the outlaws. Always on the move. Always raiding. Always more heists. Always more murders. Attacks on supply chains. Imperial forts. Tsuske would not be surprised if they were the ones who threw the oil on the fire to cause the other twelve to into acts of terrorism. The west was unstable, and his father had decided to marry a Higaziit. Tsuske was Higaziit. And now he was COBRA.

He still did not know why they were down here in the mines. The sombra. They had been ordered—commanded —to find whatever attracted their attention in the dark, hyperventilating crawl spaces in the underground tunnels. Yet, what could be down here that could attract the undead? *Maybe they just liked the dark, cramped spaces of the imperceptible void.*

They turned down another dark tunnel, having come across not a single sombra since entering this damnable place. He felt a hand on his shoulder, and he turned to face Nileen.

"This place is empty. Nothing is here."

"That is not possible, we heard the mourning of the sombra. Something has to be here."

"Will you listen for once, Tsuske? I said nothing is here. Look around you. Its empty. It's quiet."

Tsuske closed his mouth. And he listened. He could hear something, something loud and indicative. It was his heart in his ears. He was, excruciatingly, still alive. Then he heard something more, beyond his ears. Nothing. A nothingness. He sighed. "You're right. I think this place is empty."

"Back outside, we heard the cries," Dmytro said. "But they are not in here. The reports say that the sombra come in here. Follow people around. And wait for those little canaries that would die when a gas pocket popped. Then wait for the people to die. Blocking exits with their imperfect physical bodies."

"Not harming," Nileen said, "but preventing escape. Causing deaths."

"It is interesting, how they can go from translucent to physical."

"The scientist needs to figure that out," Nileen said.

"All right," Tsuske said, gesturing for the other two to be silent. "I don't like it in here anymore than you two. I'm looking for suggestions. Should we venture further in the mines and see what's down here? Or should we go back up and see what's up there?"

"This is why I am not a boss and declined the position of Second," Nileen said. "I don't like making these calls.

Tsuske looked at Dmytro who only shrugged and then seemed to bend over to pick something up off the ground. A colorful rock. Nothing important.

"The last I looked, there hadn't been an audition," Tsuske said wryly to Nileen.

"Well, there should have been because I would have turned it down."

He shook his head at her and then stared across the dark chamber and down into the tunnels. A slight breeze blew from that end of the chamber. The light from the lantern only hitting the round opening to the tunnels, appearing as holes to bottomless pits. A cold, haunting wind. Something eerie told him that if they ventured down that way, they would not be making it out tonight. Or ever.

"Let's go topside," he said, feeling his insides twist and the words coward whispered into his ears. Am I fleeing from death? he thought. "Let's go check out why the undead were making all that commotion." No, he told himself. I just don't want the people I care about to die, tonight. That is all.

As they left, thoughts still filled his mind. If that was true, why did he feel like a coward just then?

14

TSUSKE

He smirked dully, still staring back at the entrance to the rock in front of him. They had crawled up from the middle of the mines, covered in soot and smelling like earth. The rain continued to fall, and his boots sank into the quagmire the courtyard had become. Cool water droplets splashed against his exposed skin, gooseflesh across his flesh formed where they struck, creating a rippling pattern down his skin. The rain had become louder since they had gone inside, and he did not hear any of sounds other than the patter of rainfall.

They couldn't run. Climbing up the slopes had taken an awful long time, much longer than it had going down into the mines. The slopes were littered heavily with stones to help give foot leverage for the miners, and to keep wagons from sticking in the mud. When the rain became horrible, they would use flat wooden boards.

With heavy deluge, the quagmire of the mines could become a trap if the sombra and the wraith paid them a visit. Stop thinking like that, he told himself. They don't attack people. They have no reason to hurt us! His mind flashed to the memory of the black tentacle coiled around his body, releasing him, a distant scream filling his ears as he fell, rows of serrated teeth rushing up to meet him. Gooseflesh pricked his skin. Wait, he thought. Serrated or spiny? He could not remember. They were sharp, white and looked like little daggers.

"Tsuske," Nileen called to him.

He rushed to her, or tried to, his feet pulling from the mud with a loud, wet, sucking sound. "What is it?" he asked as he came near. He wasn't worried that his voice would carry, not in this torrent, but it didn't feel right to be shouting in the middle of the night, in the middle of a mission.

"You look like you're about to kill someone," she noted, seeing his appearance. "Or maybe, you just look like a wet dog."

"You said my name. What is it? What's wrong?"

"What? Nothing is wrong. Don't be a fool."

Tsuske frowned at her. Then why had she called to him? He had been busy. Busy with what? He glanced back towards the entrance of the mines, the dark entrance beckoning to him.

"It's just," she began in a soft voice. "My father, who was the king of Katar before he died—just so you know—said that there were two kinds of people in this world. Those who take lives. Then there were those who saved lives. He wanted me to be the latter. I had been destined to rule." She sighed heavily before continuing, "But then my father was killed, his brother becoming ruler, and marrying my mother. Adding her to his harem of other wives and having a million sons. You don't want to know what happens to daughters in Katar. There are a lot more men than there are women. With my brothers and sisters slain, I faked my death. Director Voren found me after a mission."

"Why are you telling me this, now?"

"Because," she said, waving a finger at him. "He told me that a great ruler, one who uplifted his people and granted mercy, saving lives, was better than one who was cruel and merciless.."

He avoided looking at her. "There isn't anything we can do to change that. No point in thinking about it."

"Of course, there is!" She growled. "Think about it. We cannot control our lives, but we can control how we are towards others. We may have a ruthless ruler, one who can kill us with a crook of his finger, but we need not let that aspect rule our hearts."

"I'm not really sure why you're telling me this."

"I think you need to hear it. Don't let your past ruin how you are in the now and the future. Only you can dictate your actions and only you have control over your heart. Do you let it remain chained and ruled by another, or do you take control of it?"

"I am loyal to the emperor and to the family line."

"We all are. But does he rule your emotions and your mind? That makes up your heart. Makes up who you are, on the inside."

Tsuske wasn't sure. He knew that he couldn't trust himself to speak just now. The night was dark, cool, and the wetness was saturating his clothes. He wore his night coat —his assignment cloak—but he could feel his limbs begin to drag. He had been up for over forty hours. He resisted the temptation to rub at his eyes.

"You know," he said, suddenly. "You should stop being be sanctimonious. It makes you look like a hypocrite."

"What?" She turned on him. "What the hell does that mean?"

"Look at you. Speaking as if you walked one who has lived a pious life. Did you not treat that Athaian woman with disdain? Like a rat or a bug under your foot while she was our captive?" She blinked at his words and seemed taken aback. "You need to remember that you are a snake, as much as I am a snake. You're no longer your father's daughter. We don't know morals; we have no ethics. We have no honor. We think and we do as the emperor demands of us and no less." He began moving away from her, she followed close by, their feet making the sucking splashing sound of a plunger pumping a latrine.

They walked in silence for a short time. She shook her head at him and breathed out slowly. More like a sigh of regret. He could tell that she, like him, fought her thoughts. "You're right. I did not like her. Still don't know if I do. But you know what? I think now I don't know what to think about what I was told. My people believed them to be witches, but then again, that was my father's brothers' doing. Are they witches? Are they the reason for all these hada we see? I don't know. What I know is that she changed me, somehow. Either influence or corrupted by her, I don't know which. I've been changed. I think," she paused, biting her lip before staring at him with hard eyes. "I think out of all of us, you've been changed the most. For better or worse."

He stopped and turned back to her. Studying her face, trying to find the condemnation that he felt by those words and only saw sympathy.

"Now, where is Dima at? Have you seen him? I think I'll go find him."

Tsuske watched her go, feeling numb.

Then he turned back towards the dark entrance, wondering what exactly was down there and what was he running from?

15

TSUSKE

R ain fell in sheets. The wind strong, whipping their cloaks around them. It was a wet, dreary night. He followed Nileen on her hunt to locate Dmytro. He had last been seen going around the industrial plant, to check out the workers and to find if something was amiss. Vanishing sombra was not unheard of but from their latest discoveries, it bode unease.

"Have you tried the comm?" Tsuske asked.

"No, I wanted to walk in mud because I find it fun. Of course, I tried the comm. You can try, see if he hears you and not me."

Tsuske had thought about that, but the way she said it meant that he would be a halfwit if he did not trust her. He was Second in command, checking would be part of his duty, however it was also noteworthy of someone of authority to trust his subordinates, even when they acted and behaved errant.

They passed through the dim lumberyard, hunched

against the wind, beneath sodden clothes. Branches once neatly thrown into a pile, now lay scattered about like the droppings of a war bird. Autumnal Fall leaves mixed with the mud had created uneven ground to trod on. Rain plastered leaves to the lower half of the buildings with thick mud layer. Tsuske splashed through puddles that chilled and numb his feet.

Waves of icy wind struck him, throwing back the hood of the cloak, wetting his hair, dripping down the side of his face and into the damp clothes underneath. They walked through the rain to the south side of the lumberyard where some people tried to work. Workers in shabby rags and shoes that were barely more than sandals tried to throw tarps over logs they had secured.

"Where could he have gotten off to?" Nileen said.

They reached the other side of the courtyard, wind-driven rain pelting their faces as if trying to push them back towards the haunting whispers of the mines. One of the workers finally noticed them and glanced at them without stopping his duties. Work was work, and these people from the Grotto would not stop working even if the sky decided to burn and fragments of the stars above smashed into the ground. To stop production meant losing work. And no one wanted to chance losing the bread and mead of their daily lives.

"Who are you? You don't look like production management. Night watchmen?"

"We are not with the Constabulary," Tsuske said, quietly. His voice would be barely audible over the rainfall and wind.

The laborer stared at him. Then looked at his dark cloak and somber appearance. The man's mood seemed to tense, knowing who he was standing before. His hands moved to his sides and Tsuske's alarm grew. He sensed Nileen stiffen. There had been rebellion in the west and some minor upstarts down here in the Grotto—nothing that the empire couldn't put to rest. People were growing cautious of strange folk, and no one enjoyed confronting a snake.

The man lowered his hand, pulling something from his work uniform, old with age and torn with holes. "I think this might belong to you?"

Nileen's hand shot out like a viper, snatching whatever it was out from the man's hands. "Where did you get this?"

"I found it in the mud," the man said.

Tsuske stared at her hands, at what was clenched in her fist. The dangling wire pieces, the ear comm and mic. He frowned. That was a comm unit.

"Damn you! I'll have you strung up if you've hurt him!"

"I promise, I only found in the mud." He backed away; his arms raised in capitulation. "I didn't—I don't know what you mean. It was just in the mud. Over there." He pointed at the ground littered with wet leaves near some logs of wood that had been tarped off.

"How did you come by it then? He wouldn't have just dropped his comm unit. You had something to do with this." Nileen stepped forward—so much talk for having control over one's emotions and mind and talk of sympathy—and he put his hand out before her, halting her approach.

"Easy, agent." Gently, he pushed her back and took a

step forward, toward the man. "Tell us what you know and what you might have seen."

"I—I didn't. I—I don't know nothing."

Tsuske continued towards the laborer.

"Rotz might have seen something. He might've. Let me call for him, eh? He's just around the corner. Over there at the other side of the logs."

"We'll be right behind you. Get him."

The mud splashed and flew as the man turned and ran towards the other end of the pile. The ends of the tarp flew, whipping in the wind, creating a cacophonous boom like a thunderclap. The other man was pulling on something and Tsuske noted that it was another person's arm, gesturing down the length of the log.

Together they stepped towards the man that the laborer had been pulling and gesturing. Going unnoticed, the man struck at his coworkers, sending him sprawling onto the wet courtyard.

"I said get off me, Clythe."

The man on the ground, his arms up in mud, left dirty trails on his already spoiled trouser bottoms as he rose to his feet. "Rotz, listen to me. These agents wish to speak with you."

"What agents? I don't see any..." the man called Rotz trailed off as he stared at Tsuske and Nileen.

And then turned and he ran.

AND THEY GAVE CHASE.

Running through the backwater roads, the assailant was right in front of them. Never slowing his pace, he seemed to run off of the shadows of the night. Seeming to stay ahead of them.

They emerged along a busy main thoroughfare of the market district known as the Bizarre and into the crowds of the night. People did not sleep down in the Grotto as much as they did not sleep up topside. For the Gestahlians, that was due to privilege of birth; being able to stay up and enjoy their decadent lifestyle. These people were awake so they could survive.

As their hasty approach towards the districts nearest the central spiral, the rain suddenly stopped. The closer the neighborhoods go to the apex of the lower grotto that had been built right beneath the upper city, the less precipitation would be seen.

The man they gave chase to had disappeared amongst the crowds.

Tsuske prowled through the market, cloak pulled low, hands at his sides, ready to pull forth any number of artillery to apprehend the suspect. Nileen scanned the crowds. Nobody else seemed to have noticed them or the man they were chasing.

"Where did he go?" Nileen asked.

"I don't know." A growing unease filled him. Was this a rebel, an insurgent from the west and had they somehow captured one of the COBRA—an elite assassin of the empire. An enemy that had outpaced, out maneuvered and outran them just now?

"I think we need to split up."

"Agreed. You take west quadrant, and I'll patrol east. He could not have gone south or north."

"Sounds good to me." And then he was alone. Nileen disappearing into the crowds.

Regular shipments of supplies from the south and north, had set the market bustling. Fortunately for them, at all times of the day and night, the roads were packed full of bustling farmers from the south or dock workers from the north, bringing in goods. Besides carts and the sometimes one-manned pullers, a running man would have been noticed on the busy streets north and south. That could only indicate that the runner had gone left or right.

Commerce. People so low that the homes they lived in had dirt floors, these people survived off of money. With the continual supply trains and wagons from the south bringing in agricultural goods and the sailors bringing in goods from the port, it created a hectic atmosphere. Money exchanged hands, golds, silvers and coppers. The need for trade was proof that bargaining and jobs would persist.

Delivery, handling goods, unloading and reloading, street cleaners that stood ready with a pale and a shovel to clean up the mess of the wagon animals or the food animals that had were brought to market. No matter what time trade happened, there would be people willing to buy and people looking for the next gig to survive on for another day. Even in the rain, the people would find themselves coming out into the open city of the Grotto. And how much more people there would be during day rise? Too many.

Lurking within it all, somewhere, was the man that

Tsuske and Nileen were after. A man that knew something of the disappearance of Dmytro. He thought he heard laughter, coming from a distant place as he stood in the middle of the street, crowds steering around him as he remained still, listening. The din of voices, people shouting, and animals braying was overwhelming. And then there was the raucous laughter, the kind that comes from when money is spent too much on drink.

How could they laugh while doing commerce during this time of night... and while that a fugitive was on the run?

They don't know about that, Tsuske reminded himself. And likely, they would cheer for him. The people were loyal to the empire—they had to be; they've been indoctrinating since birth to believe it was just. The people would continue to live in squalor beneath the emperor as they believe it was what the gods wanted for them and yet they would root for the underdog who evaded the law. How loyal can a person be if they were the root of the rebellion and the troubles the empire faced?

Maybe it was not the people who were the problem. Was that his thought or somebody else's?

Tsuske was conflicted and he shoved the treasonous thoughts down. *Best to not think about it.*

It had been a frustrating night and Tsuske could feel himself going dry from the buzz of the alcohol he had consumed earlier. He rarely drank, if ever, and now he wanted to return to it after the night was over.

Dmytro first. Then to the emperor. Then maybe sleep. *Yes, sleep sounds good.*

He searched the streets, his feet splashing through puddles, and inquired with Nileen if she had found anything. So far, they found nothing. She was just as tired as he was, both suffering from the long night and the previous day's excursions. Fortunately, Tsuske did not have a life outside doing the bidding for the lord emperor—so he should not suffer for it.

Practiced training with the squad—more like listening to Nileen and Director Voren bicker and get into heated discussions on morality or terminology usage regarding the directors favored anecdotal analogies. The occasional meetings where he sat in with the lord emperor and the director, and the other elites as they discussed historical records and important information regarding the safety and security of Gestahl. Tsuske's life revolved around the empire.

Tsuske was second in command of COBRA and next in line to lead after Director Voren. And what a distant he felt between himself and the man in charge of the snakes. Director Voren was a leader; one who showed, by example, increasing patrols, with strict rules of conduct and integrity. Though he was not always professional amongst his close crew, they saw him as an executive amongst the elite and the other fellow snakes. One to follow by his example. With him injured, Tsuske was now in charge. But why did he feel anything but in control? Where were these doubts coming from?

He wanted more than a vague but definitive explanation of the orders he was assigned and commanding of his fellow COBRA—but those were the very soul of being an assassin. You do as you're told, don't ask for explanations, don't question. And at the same time, it required you to provide distinct intelligence.

"Six coppers and no more."

"Done, I'll take the boar as well."

"Dressed or fresh?"

"Fresh."

"Three silvers for the boar."

Tsuske listened to the voices of the marketplace and the ripple of wind against window shutters and flags declaring loyalty or wares. His foot hit the broken cement ground as he crossed another street. As he stepped foot onto the walkway, something changed. Abruptly, sound ceased for just a moment. As if a hand covered his ears and then relinquished their hold.

The wind had silenced. The laughter had vanished. He had the sudden feeling of being watched.

He stopped and turned, listening. Watching. Observing.

"Not again," a merchant said above the noise of the crowd. "You're not welcome here. Not you. Go on now."

"The urchins come out even at night."

"They're lucky no one has picked one of them up."

"If you see one, undoubtedly there is an entire group of them nearby."

"Two coppers for the apple. More equals less spent. Six coppers for the four."

"Hey, you, you're not welcome here. Go before I call for the Constabulary."

"Too many patrols out tonight. I wonder what is going on?"

"There are a lot of soldiers out tonight patrolling the southern agricultural districts."

"I hear that the sombra are on the move."

"On the move? They always seem to be around nowadays. Annoying little beasties."

"Beasts? They are supposed to be our ancestry spirits."

"I believe that. I once saw my dead aunt walking about —took the empire an entire fleet to send her back to rest. She was definitely a beast in real life."

Even the people had noticed the increase in the number of the soulless ones. The undead. The sombra. Before Tsuske and his team of COBRA went to the north, the sombra had begun to act strange. As if they were waiting for something to occur. Lurking around the corner. Getting in the way. More and more of their number had been seen.

A month ago, a friendly game of dice had turned to violence, and one player had hit another over the head with an empty tankard. Tavern fights were not ordinarily lethal, but in that instance it had not been the bottle that had killed the poor fellow. It had been the ground that had waited to meet the man's head that had done him in. Striking his head at the corner of the table, doing him in. The guards had been called to haul off the perpetrator. When the incinerators were called in, they had arrived, and the body was simply gone. The tavern folk had said that the man just got up and walked again, seemingly uninjured; disappearing into the night. A sombra had been seen at the time, lurking around the building. Another had been seen in that same tavern, floating between the floorboards and into melting into the walls.

Had they planned the man's death? He wondered. *No, impossible. They're soulless, they're without wits. Planning is what the living do.*

But he couldn't help but wonder.

There had been a series of unfortunate events since then involving the soulless, despite the lord emperor blaming the COBRA for bringing back sombra into Gestahl. And as unfortunate as they were, it was something he had been hoping for tonight. Something to indicate that the sombra were changing—that the prior incidents were not just spoofs. That they had not brought the sombra into the upper city. That something was attracting their attention.

Now… he watched. He searched. And he waited.

The wind seemed to calm.

The sombra had been acting strangely. Could whoever had taken Dmytro be tied into it? Or was it just a coincidence?

"The attack will come," a passerby said. "Watch yourselves."

An otherworldly laugh echoed in his mind.

The voice had come from where? Tsuske looked around, trying to determine where the laughter originated.

OVER HERE. The voice crooned.

Tsuske watched the crowds while idly touching the holster to his side arms. Would he fire into a crowd? No, something less obvious but just as lethal. Tsuske enjoyed watching people. Watching, thinking. Enjoying the experiences that other's could have. Tsuske flipped one of his hidden knives up from the concealed part of his cloak and caught it, then spun the weapons between his fingers as he searched.

Where had the voice come from?

OVER HERE.

There! A shadow moved. A man's face appeared between two shopkeeper's tents. The one they were seeking. He had been watching Tsuske.

Then the man turned and ran. Again.

Finally, Tsuske thought, *I have you now.*

Catching the knife, he gave chase. The fugitive barreled through the crowd, missing everyone in his path. Tsuske charged after, narrowly avoiding colliding into the oncoming traffic of the nightlife.

Tsuske was hot in pursuit, his heart beating violently. If he failed the chase, he'd have to report his mistakes. His failures. He could not fail again—if he was even given that chance. The man would hide, and Tsuske had a feeling that this was the last chance he would have. He also had the feeling the lord emperor wanted him to fail tonight. Wanted to execute him.

And he just might fail in the mission. But not in this, not in locating the whereabouts of his comrade. I can't fail now!

He sprinted down an alley, leaving behind the more populated sections of the main thoroughfare. The alley was dark and void of street lights, broken cardboard boxes and refuse lay against the edifice of the buildings. Eyes of the street urchins and homeless fell onto them—and they were not kind. They were dim with lackluster, only those who had nothing else to look forward to, had. The eyes of the hopeless.

His hand touched the comm unit on his ear. "Nileen. North corridor. Past pike. I'm hot in pursuit. Got a visual."

"Got it. I'm heading your way. I'll try to cut him off."

The chase led him deeper into the far reaches of the back streets, to areas where the Constabulary would only be seen patrolling in groups. Where the streets became less straight and less uniformed. The heart of where the citizens lived.

The man run as if he were not human. Tsuske could hear his own breathing coming in and out, the splash of his boots into the muddy puddles underfoot, the cries of the orphans and the weeping of those who experienced this hell every day.

The man up ahead stopped. Tsuske slowed and stopped when he was several meters away.

"Put your hands in the air and turn slowly. I have some questions for you."

The man did not move. Cool wetness splashed his face as the winds changed their course, bringing the deluge back this way once again. And still, the man did not react.

"I said, put your hands in the air and turn slowly. I will kill you if I have to, whether or not I get answers. We have fingers prints of every citizen on file and can find the information I require by other means. Don't make this hard on yourself." He pulled out one of his lights, and the glow of light seemed to be sucked away, pulled as if a black hole had snared it.

Abruptly, the man fell to all fours and Tsuske wondered

if he had been hurt. Then he crawled—frantic—until he reached the alley wall and.. slowly disappeared right in front of his eyes. Tsuske rushed forward. Had the fugitive found a sewer tunnel to crawl into? No, not that. The man —the thing—was squeezing into a hold in the wall about a foot wide in broken angles.

"What the hell?"

Head and hands were already gone, legs kicked furtively until they too disappeared out of sight. Tsuske bent down to peer into the hole, careful not to get too close to whatever that was. And saw a pair of red eyes staring back at him and a wicked serrated smile.

16

TSUSKE

The man had disappeared into a hole. Squeezing himself into a hole in the wall, a hole that had possibly been made by protests that had occurred recently or in the past. What the hell was that thing?

"Nileen," Tsuske said into the comm. "I don't think this is a man we're after."

"What do you mean?" She answered back, her breath coming in a huff.

"The fugitive squeezed into a tiny hole in the wall."

The other end was silent for a moment. "That doesn't sound right. Could it be a soulless? One of the sombra?"

"Have they been known to do that?"

"In their mindless bodies, yeah."

"But when they claim host over a body? This thing acted human and yet—it squeezed into a wall."

"I don't know what that was. Doesn't sound like anything we have ever dealt with. I'm almost there. Rounding the corner and be there shortly."

Tsuske let out his breath. The chase had ended in a dead end. Where could Dmytro be? What the hell was going on?

Nileen came charging into the alley and ran up to meet him.

"That's the hole?" She asked, breathlessly. Her hands on her hips as she gathered her breath and stared at the damaged wall.

"Yep, that is the one."

"Damn. What the hell is going on here?"

"I don't know. Something's wrong."

"Where the hell did they take Dmytro?" Nileen demanded.

Tsuske didn't have an answer for her. For he, too, did not know. Nothing was making sense. They were supposed to dispatch the undead. Lure them away, but a man had showed up and lured them away from the mines. Was the answer inside the mines? He realized that he had left the pack and cage that held the dying animal back at the mines. Curse him for a fool.

A soft sound, a scuttle of a boot against the pavement, caught his attention. He looked up and realized he had been staring at the hole. The hole that reminded him of the entrance of the mines. Dark and brooding, with answers right out of sight.

"Who's there?" Nileen called.

A little girl stepped forward, pale, sickly and very dirty. Her dark brown hair looked to have grown in different spurts of growth or had been cut unevenly. Mats of hair clung to each other as if the young child had not brushed in a very long time—if ever. Honey brown eyes stared up at them.

"Do you have food?" the soft voiced said. "I am hungry." She wore dirty brown trousers and a man's shirt that went well past her waist. Her bare feet dug into the slime of the back alley they were in.

Pity hit his gut. Despite being COBRA, he could not help but have sympathy for the street urchins. Those who remained uncaught often died worse lives than those who were captured and brought to the tower. He wondered if he should call dispatch to come take a patrol down this alley, root up all the homeless and the unwanted.

"Don't pity her, Tsuske," Nileen said, roughly. "She is not here for that, are you? What do you got, little one?"

Tsuske shot her a frown at how she spoke to the child, but the little girl turned away from him and looked... playful. If that could be the right word. Eager? "I know things." She twiddled with a strand of hair between her fingers. "Feed me and I will tell you what I know."

"Nu-uh. If you're that smart to know this game, child, you know that you don't get nothing unless you tell us something."

The child bit her lower lip, her face scrunched up in thought. Then she nodded. "Okay. I saw a group of people, they were strange. The guy you were chasing—he was part of that group. Said he would lay a trap for a snake. I thought, maybe, he meant the bad kind. The kinds that bite. Did he mean you guys?"

Tsuske frowned. "What do you mean?"

Nileen shot him an exasperated look but then nodded toward the girl to answer.

"I thought I would get something after I told you something." The child fidgeted with something in her hands. A small white broken doll not her hair, Tsuske realized. Only the arms, head and burnt hair remained. The face was unrecognizable. Possibly it had been running over by a wagon and then fallen against a fire.

"She is right. Here, I tend to carry chocolate on me. Do you like chocolate?" Nileen pulled something out from within her cloak. A cloth with a ribbon tied around it. Neatly, she untied the bow string and opened the bundle. Soft white, irregularly sized chunks sat in her palm. "Do you want one?"

"I—I want it all."

"Only after you tell us what you know. All of it for all of this."

The little girl licked her lips. "Can I have one now?"

"No, no. You can wait. But I promise you can have this entire bag for yourself, chocolate and bag. You can carry stuff inside this bag. Even a cute little bow for your doll."

"I can have that, too?"

"Everything here," Nileen said, gently.

"The men said they would trap some snakes. They would get some undead, too. Not sure how because the spirits move through walls and don't seem to listen." Then, thoughtfully, the girl smiled and said, "One of them had a large knife. And his eyes were strange."

"A soulless held a knife?" Tsuske said. "Ordinarily they just go about their merry time in a new body."

"Not these," the child said in a not too soft voice. "They're different."

"How do you know that?" Nileen asked.

The girl gestured towards the wall with her doll and then stroked the doll. Soothing it. "They crawl through things they shouldn't be able to do. Climb things they shouldn't be able to. They bother some of us and don't seem very nice. They're not very kind or silly like the sombra are."

"It's because the sombra are not kind or silly," Tsuske said none too gently. "You do not want to mess with them."

"Maybe, but there isn't much to do around here. They can be fun to play with."

"Child, do you know where those men were heading?"

The girl bit her lip and extended her free hand. "Give me the bag and I will tell you."

"Little brat," Tsuske whispered under his breath. Admiring her audacity.

"No, look here, I said after you told us, I'll give it to you."

"No," the girl said strongly. "I want it now!" She stomped her foot for emphasis.

Nileen shot him a look, and he only shrugged. Sighing, she tied up the bag and then walked towards the girl.

"No!" The girl said with abruptness, urgency in her voice. "Put it on the ground and back away. I don't want you to come closer. I don't want you taking me away."

"All right, fine." Nileen bent over and placed the cloth bag on the ground, on the nearest part that she could see that was not soaked.

The girl jumped at the bag and then was on her feet

again, backing away. Not taking her light brown eyes from them. Her feet looked toughened and ragged from being on the street for so long barefoot.

"Hey, now. Tell us what we want to know."

Loosening the bow, the girl stuck her dirty hands into the bag and pulled out a soft white chunk before tossing it into her mouth. For one still moment, the child seemed to become the young person that stood before them. Eyes closed. A blissful smile spreading over her face as she moved the decadent morsel from one cheek to the other, the smile never leaving her face.

"They were heading towards the industrial district." And then she turned and ran, her bare feet splashing in the water the rain had left that. Tsuske looked up and noticed that the rain had finally stopped.

17

TSUSKE

They made their way towards the industrial district where the mining industry was located. An area of factories and where the mass production of goods were manufactured. Tannery, leatherworkers, smithies, glassblowers and the works. And the mines.

As they wound their ways away from the central markets, and further out, the wind picked up.

He had lost hope as they reached the end of the street at an intersection and continued down another less traversed road. If he was feeling this way, he could only imagine what Nileen was feeling since she seemed to be his polar opposite. He glanced at her and saw her look of fierce determination. She saw and smiled at him.

"We will find him. And we will fry whoever took him."

"This will not look good," Tsuske said.

"Who cares? I'm ready to roast someone's ass right now." Her brow furrowed as she studied his face. "Why do you look so thoughtful?"

"Trying to think of answers for the future conversations we will have with the echelons."

"Don't worry about that right now. Dmytro is who should be on our minds."

"You think about him enough for the both of us. Let me think what I need to think."

"Right, about that, let's just wing it. We'll be killing a few tonight, and that always makes the Lord Emperor smile down upon us."

Tsuske sighed. That was true. "You're right. I'll keep my mind on our current objective."

"That's what I am talking about. Mind on Dima."

"No," Tsuske said. "The Lord Emperor wanted us to bring back the sombra who assaulted us earlier or bring back whatever it is they're after."

Nileen scoffed. "Yeah—but Dima—"

"He will be all right. He is a COBRA. He can handle himself, even when the odds are against him."

Nileen remained silent. She did not seem to like his answer.

"And we'll need to report the location of the urchins and the homeless we saw tonight."

"I didn't see anything," Nileen said. She had a stubborn look on her face.

"No? And what do you think that girl was?"

"Lost. Confused. Not an urchin. She's a person. And she was right to fear us. Shoot, I fear us sometimes."

Tsuske looked at her with understanding. "Yeah— everyone should fear us. Even ourselves."

"I don't think we should report it, Tsuske."

"We have to. It's part of our duty."

"No, it isn't. We can let that slide."

"Do you really think being a street child, an orphan like that, is any better than being brought in?"

"Do you really think captivity and life in a laboratory, no matter how short, is even better?"

"They have food. They have comfort. Better than naked and starving. You didn't see the people in that alley. They're wet. They're hungry and cold. They're miserable."

"And a cage is better?" Nileen asked genuinely.

"They're provided for until humanely put down. Their usefulness to the empire gives them honor. It is the law to report orphans and vagabonds. It is the law to be of use in the empire. There is always work to be done."

Nileen shook her head. "I'm asking you not to report it. Just this one time. I have a hunch that it's the wrong choice to make."

"Why do you say that? Is it because you're feeling guilty over the Athaian woman's captivity?" Tsuske asked. Clarity hit him in the gut and wanted to wrench his heart out. Was that the source of his problem? *Am I feeling... remorse? No. That couldn't be it.* Higaziit do not feel remorseful for their actions. They're traitors. He was a traitor. A traitor feeling traitorous feelings.

Her eyes widened at him and she nodded her head. "And you feel it too."

"Come on," Tsuske said. "We're not far. Let's go get the bad guys and bring home our friend."

"Now you are talking."

The mines were a fenced off area, expansive, covering over a mile of digging. A deep hundred-meter hole in the ground, with sloping slides. Foot paths where wagons coming to and from with deposits could traverse, making their way from the bottom of the ravine to the top where some buildings occupied. The bright lights of the lit lanterns gave the courtyard light, but the pit in the distanced hovered in the darkness. The darkness seemed to be pulsing. Had it been like that the first time they had come here, earlier in the night?

"How did we go up those slopes in the rain and wind earlier and still have energy to make it this far in the night?" Nileen asked. "The wind is still, and it's not even raining anymore and I'm feeling exhausted."

"Quiet," Tsuske said. "Looks like no one is here. Let's scout out a good look out area and wait for the targets to arrive." They split up. Tsuske tested his hands on the window ledge of the nearest building. Part of the building had a low terrace; one he could easily scale and take cover on.

"First thing I'll do when Dmytro is back is go get a hard apple cider. Hot. Has to be hot."

"No, the first thing you will do is to be quiet." He pulled himself to the roof and lay down. It was wet.

"I was talking about afterwards. You are so dense sometimes." But she fell into silence.

They waited like that for quite some time. The darkness

of the void of the pit seemed to grow as Tsuske's eyes adjusted to the light of the surrounding lamp posts. The lower half of the buildings had brightly lit lanterns along the walls. A requirement that the empire had issued for industrial buildings. Workers had to have a well-lit work environment. Even though the mines had been abandoned for a short time now, lantern workers would come in and light the area.

A noise alerted him to trespassers down below. Holding his breath, he lay on the roof; he scooted to the edge and watched as two individuals crept into the courtyard.

"The lights are lit."

"Told you they had been. We didn't forget."

"I just wanted to make sure."

"See? We're done here. I don't even know why we have to keep the damn place lit. No workers to be seen here."

"Well, I guess we're done for the night then."

The pair left as quickly as they had come, and Tsuske listened to their footfall disappear before he sat up. Touching his comm unit, he said, "Nileen, I don't think they're coming. I think, perhaps, they're in the mines."

"You think so?"

"Yeah. Think about it. That girl said a group of them had said they were coming this way. But that was a while back, and we must have been here during that time."

"You think, maybe they arrived just as we were leaving?"

"I don't know how we missed them or how they snuck up on Dmytro, but I think they're down there. Waiting for us."

"A trap then."

"An ambush, no doubt." He lowered himself from the ledge and rendezvoused with Nileen.

"Tsuske," Nileen said. "You realize that these are sombra we are talking about. Not people anymore."

"I know," he said. Ice ran up his back. Sombra, mindless entities or spirits. When they possessed a body, they behaved and acted like the person the body had once been. But then… they shouldn't be able to squeeze through holes the length of a knife. "They're changing. Somehow. We need to bring one in, if possible. I think that would make the lord emperor happy."

"But Tsuske—"

"I know, Dmytro comes first. If it's possible, we need to bring one in."

"But Tsuske—I think we aren't dealing with an entire group of soulless. I think people are mixed up in this somehow, in some way. If we even try to bring that thing in, someone is going to get hurt. Could be Dmytro."

Tsuske thought about it and agreed. "Yeah, you're right. There may be casualties tonight. We'll be careful, but you know we need to bring it in."

"Killing these things is nearly impossible. Bringing one of these changed things in, will be damn near impossible, too. I don't want to risk Dima."

"We have little choice, Nileen." She opened her mouth, and he raised a hand to forestall her protest. "I've been thinking about that and I think I have an idea."

"What're you suggesting? We go in there with our guns and daggers out?"

"No, it might be a little more interesting than that."

Tsuske looked towards the cage he had left by the wall earlier in the night. No doubt the thing inside was dead. Nileen looked and then catching on, she smiled and nodded her understanding.

Things were about to get a lot more interesting... and a lot more dangerous.

18

TSUSKE

The thing had not yet died.

Tsuske looked into the folds of the cloth-covered cage and squinted his eyes. Nope, it was still alive and kicking. Tentacles wiggled about a bulbous head protectively as a pale blue fluid drizzled onto the cage bottom.

"Don't harass it Tsuske. It knows it's going to die, soon."

"It knows nothing at all, Nileen. It's just a plant."

"A living plant."

"All plants are living."

"This species is different. They feel pain."

"Unlikely. It's a plant. It doesn't have feelings or the brain to allow it such emotions. It's just a carnivorous plant. One that will bite when threatened."

"When feeling threatened? Perhaps it feels that it should bite because its feels threatened. I feel that makes sense."

"You don't want to know what I am feeling right now," Tsuske said.

Nileen chuckled. "You know, where I come from, these things don't exist. Why is the east continent so full of weird things? Snakes and squirming plants with tentacles."

"The western continent has these forms of plants, too. You just don't see them because they're aquatic. The ends of those tentacles are tipped with poison. You wouldn't want to see them. This one is harmless."

"Except when full sized. They have rows of spiny looking teeth that are ready to devour their prey."

"It's why we use germinated seedlings. Sprouts."

"Right," Nileen said with disgust. "Babies. You harm baby plants to lure the sombra. Babies, Tsuske."

Tsuske rolled his eyes. He often preferred to work alone. And yet... he enjoyed working with his comrades. But sometimes... "They're a plant-animal hybrid. For whatever reason, the sombra are attracted to them. And they feel nothing."

"Oh, so now you admit that they're an animal, too? So maybe they can feel."

"Enough of that. There isn't much we can do. They're easily bred, and the thousands of seeds we get help lure sombra away from the cities. What else can we do?"

"Hmm..." Nileen mused. "You forgot that we use donkeys and other forms of quick-footed livestock to encourage the monsters outside the perimeter walls to leave the area. You must admit that they feel, too."

Tsuske didn't reply. It was either a quick-footed animal or a human. They didn't have a lot of choices to choose from.

"Do you ever wonder where they go?"

"Who?"

"The animals. We cut them on the haunch. They're wounded, but only a flesh wound. In all likelihood, they could outrun the sombra. Do you think there is an entire herd of them out there somewhere, living together? The survivors of the cuttings and the great scourge that chased them?"

"I never really thought about it. Maybe, you ought to write a book on it."

Nileen shot him a smile. "So, what do we do now?"

"Make our way into the mines. The slopes will be wet, and we need to be careful. We are heading straight into an ambush. But perhaps we can turn this around into a preemptive strike instead."

"Lead the way, boss man."

Tsuske felt a little apprehensive of those words and what they could mean for his future. Director Voren should be going through surgery right now. In a world of hope, he should make it out all right. In this world and age, Tsuske couldn't help but feel nervous at the thought the director may never make it out and that he would be placed in charged. *If I am not killed before then*, he thought wryly.

It would take a bold plan for this mission to succeed. He only hoped that his idea would be bold enough.

"WE WILL NEED to go down there."

"Now?"

Tsuske nodded. "Yes..." he stared off at the black maw of the tunnel entrance. How was it that they had gone in there earlier? His lantern light on his waist had illuminated his path on the way down as it had previously, but why did it seem to shirk away from the darkness as if it melted like ice against hot coals?

They entered the tunnels. The eerie quiet sounding louder than their own heartbeats. The silence that was not so silent. Lower they descended, like spiraling darkness, a pit that seemed to open up into the void itself. Tsuske felt his heart beginning to hammer into his chest, his hands quivered with the need to hold one of his many knives or his handgun. Yes, his fingers itched for that weapon, yearning for the protection it promised. But cannot do anything here, he told himself.

"I don't like this," Nileen said.

Neither did Tsuske.

The darkness seemed to pulse against the lanterns at their waists, trying to push back or devour the light. His memory flashed to the mountaintop; the great escape in the snow mobiles with the daemons at their backs—those had been soulless. Yet they did not act normal. They had spoken! An oddity that had never been seen before. And the surrounding darkness had seemed to hum.

As it did now.

"I hear voices," Nileen mouthed. It was true. Voices up ahead echoed down into the tunnel. Tsuske nodded to her and put a finger to his lip to show continued silence and Nileen gave him a curt, impatient nod. "I know!" It said.

The tunnel opened and up ahead. Walking shoulder to shoulder had almost been too cramped. Tsuske preferred wide space between him and his comrades. Friendly fire did not usually happen, but when it did it was likely because of the proximity of the team. The vast chamber was up ahead. Once it had been filled with deposits of minerals and ore, long ago. Now the chamber was empty, all except for the dozen of tunnels branching off from it and into other various places beneath the Grotto.

How had the Grotto not collapsed, he wondered in awe? Then scolded his wayward thoughts. Stay focused!

They turned off their lanterns as light up ahead could be seen, illuminating the tunnel entrance. Footsteps approached and passed in front of them. Tsuske and Nileen halted their descension. Whoever it was, was beyond the opening into the chamber up ahead.

"Why can't we just kill him already?" A voice said. Nileen tensed up beside him.

"You know why. The boss wants him for other means. Says he senses something about the man."

"Why not just make another sombra out of him? Like the boss."

"Idiot, you can't make a sombra out of him. It's a soulless that comes when a sombra finds a host."

"But I don't like the looks of him. The way he stares at me. Can't we do something about his eyes?"

"The boss wants him as he is. Says he senses something special about him. Don't touch him."

"But—"

"Do I have to cut off your fingers? Don't touch him."

"I wasn't going to touch him."

Tsuske and Nileen inched their way towards the entrance. There were two empty wagons up ahead. He gestured for Nileen to take lead as she carried the cage on her back. He would provide cover—what limited coverage he could against an unknown lurking enemy—that he could. Tsuske could see a body laying against a couple barrels and that two bodies stood above him as they talked.

"Good, because I isn't telling you again. Be an idiot and suffer the consequences, that's what boss used to say."

"He don't say that no more."

"Because he has changed. He has become something better." A yearning filled that man's voice. "And promises the riches for us if we cooperate. So, don't go messing things up for us."

"I am cooperating."

The two continued to bicker as Nileen and Tsuske slid behind the wagons. His eyes roamed the vast chamber. There were a lot of lights. Dozens of polls had been set with lanterns, giving the chamber a warm ambience. That is foolish, he thought. Fire in a mine? What if there is a loosed gas pocket? It provided a warm lit glow, not brightness, like the mine's interior lights, but light enough to see the chamber well enough.

"What're we doing down here, Gleb?"

"Waiting for the boss to return from his trip through the mines," Gleb said.

"Yeah, but what we doing? We could have watched the fellow up there."

"The boss wanted us down here with him."

"I don't like it down here. It's spooky."

"Don't be an idiot, Rotz. No one down here but you, me and that guy on the ground. Nothing spooky. Or are sombra spooky to you now?"

"Sombra? No. Not at all. I sort of like them."

"They're like the boss, so you had better like them."

"What is like me?" A voice sounding like wind stirring the leaves came from one of the dark tunnels called. "Are you comparing me to one of the mindless?"

"Nah boss. Just saying—"

"Silence," the voice said. An entity seemed to float into the chamber. The light coming off the taverns seemed to move around the darkness that surrounded it. Wisps of darkness broke out as tentacles that moved in around Dmytro and the two men standing near him. The tentacles seemed to be hesitant to touch the fallen man and suddenly recoiled back. That darkness seeped away and back into the mass of the shadow and then dissolved. A figure stood in the smoke, at the center of the shadow. A figure that reflected the light, like glistening tar. And then that, too, changed... and a person walked out from that writhing mass of darkness. The former shadow slipped away, leaving a man in its place.

Nileen looked with concern toward Dmytro. Tsuske rubbed his chin. He could feel the beginning stages of stubble to grow on his chin.

This was the thing that had escape into the wall, and it was also the wraith that has assaulted them in Gestahl. They had found the thing they were looking for.

WE SHOULDN'T HAVE COME HERE, his mind told him. We cannot fight this thing.

Timorous emotions poured into him as his mind witnessed the mass of darkness turn into a man. Waves of self-doubt, self-loathing, and ineptitude seemed to want to take him over. Why had they come here?

A voice, sickly sweet, whispered into his mind. You cannot take this thing on. Go back to the lord emperor. Submit your neck onto the guillotine. Admit your failure.

"Tsuske?"

A soft cry echoed in his ears. It was Maya, his little sister. A cry that turned into a scream as the crackling flames roared louder.

You are a failure, Tsuske. You killed your family. Your little sister had not even been given her true name yet before she was killed in that fire. Your mother had been pregnant. You killed her and the baby. You were the traitor. It was you all along. Your team is better off without you. Admit it. The smell of smoke and burnt flesh entered his nose, and he dry retched quietly into his arm.

"Tsuske?"

Tsuske shook. His body trembling beneath the powerful thoughts that had flooded him. Long had that memory lay dormant, forgotten. Removed from his memory by a force of will. Now it resurfaced for him to face.

"It's that thing," her voice said. "It is speaking to us in our minds."

He blinked, wrenching himself away from the vivid memories that were filling him.

Moisture dripped from his chin, and he realized he was crying. The soft cry he had heard had escaped from his own lips. He heard the raucous laughter in his ears. It enjoyed his torment.

"Boss, please, your power is too much to bear."

"I don't think I can take it anymore." A gun shot echoed through the chamber and a body fell to the ground.

"Greb! Greb! Get up, Greb. Get up! Oh, by the goddess, what have you done? Why? It's all my fault. I shouldn't have been an idiot. I'm sorry, Greb. I'm sorry." The other man fell to his knees, weeping.

WEAK MORTALS. WHEN WILL YOUR KIND EVER LEARN? the whisper sounding like the rustling of leaves.

"You promised us riches. You promised us fortunes beyond our lives are worth."

DO YOU QUESTION ME NOW, MORTAL?

"You promised… and now Greb is dead."

DEATH FOLLOW THAT OF THE WEAK. The wind hissed. THE TIME OF RECKONING IS COMING. THE PRICE OF THE REAPER'S BILL SHALL BE PAID.

The man kneeling on the ground suddenly went quiet. His sobs shut off by an invisible force.

The entity with the man's body walked forward, the body did not seem to be able to contain all the mass of the dark one's power. Smokey tendrils leaked out at the man's feet and from his back. A tentacle extended out and gently caressed the dead body. Another oily tentacle touched the bullet wound, pulling back with the end covered in blood before coming to the wraith's mouth. A long tongue licked at the ends of the dark appendage. "Until that time, you all have work to do." A man's voice this time. Warm. Almost charming.

"Good to see you, boss. Are you going to summon one of the sombra?" The man said with a tremoring voice.

The man transformed back into the wraith. Black smoke issued out from the body it occupied before imploding and vanishing. SILENCE. A tentacle streaked out across the ground and prodded Dmytro.

"But, Greb. Make him moving again, boss. Bring him back." The man sniffed and began to hiccup.

FORGET HIM. CHECK THE SNAKE'S BODY. SOMETHING IS THERE.

"But Greb told me not to touch him."

The wraith turned in the air to look at him, hissing like a striking viper. The man shrank back as if facing the opening to a chasm and feared falling over. Still whimpering, he fell to his knees again and quickly patted down Dmytro. "He still lives," he said hoarsely, as his hand came resting on Dmytro's neck.

WHAT IS ON HIS BODY? TELL ME.

"Guns. I feel some knives. And," his voice trembling as he spoke, "some rocks. Just rocks."

ROCKS? FOOL. THOSE ARE NO ROCKS. THOSE HOLD REMNANTS OF LIGHT. AH—THAT WAS WHAT HE CARRIED. KILL HIM NOW.

With a sinking feeling, Tsuske felt for his weapons, readying himself. He could taste the old air in the chamber.

His foot nudged at a pile of rocks and splinters of wood, creating a soft scattering sound that seemed to echo like thunder in his ears.

WE HAVE VISITORS.

The darkness seeped down from the tunnels, into the vast chamber like puffs of black clouds. It wasn't fast, but there was an inexorable way it moved, flowing up the sides of the walls, towards the ceiling. On the floor below, shadows swirled with violet colors streaked with black smoke as shapes took form. Moans filled the room as arms reached through the wrenches in the ground, figures pulling themselves up from the deep void. Their forms rippled and threatened to vanish like the smoke that they were made of. Despite that, the bodies kept coming up from the ground, growing in number.

"This is not good," Nileen said.

With his back against the wagon wheel, his legs underneath him, Tsuske nodded. "We need a good plan. Give me the cage and you go dispatch the idiot and rescue Dmytro." She looked ready to protest, but she must have seen the look in his eyes that would bear no further argument. She unslung the leather straps and set the cage down quietly before nodding and turning away from him.

Forward. He rose, brushing off his knees, which only reminded him he might die here, anyway. If you're going to die, die for a comrade.

That felt right.

Grabbing the leather straps, he slung the cage upon his back, feeling the weight settle on his shoulders. The thing inside barely moved as he shifted his weight. He stepped out from behind the wagon, the large rusty one with the broken wheel just as Nileen crept around the other side and out of sight.

"I see we meet again, soulless one." His voice was barely above a whisper, but his voice had carried. He kept his hands at his sides, the weight of the cage upon his back, the thick straps pressing in around his shoulders.

The undead... look like us, Tsuske thought as he watched the group of sombra moved in around the dead body but did not go in for the claim. A dark coil, writhing in smoke, had twisted around the dead body, slowing dragging it back towards its master. The wraith.

"I know you need not speak with your mouth to convey your thoughts to me. I heard you earlier, up in the streets. That was you, whispering my name, wasn't it?"

The clothing—if that is what it was called—rippled as if an unseen hand trailed its fingers through its contrails. The eyes of the daemon glowed a menacing red. The body on the ground continued to be pulled closer, arms sprawled out, picking up dust as it moved.

The sombra filed in behind him, occluding the only exit out of the vast chamber and crowding the room with their presence. The mouths they formed, sprouting spiny teeth. A tension filled the room. A waiting. The feeling was of a pack of animals surrounding a wounded beast, knowing they had the greater number.

There would be no escape.

Steeling his spine, he stood in front of the wraith whom towered high above him, never having faced a mortal who braved that deathly stare. His legs threatened to cower before this mighty entity, the voices and howling whispered in his mind, crooning their woe of failure. He brushed it aside with difficulty. He was Higaziit. He knew difficulties.

"What the hell—" the voice stammered as it broke off into a wet guttural sound, gurgling and bubbly. A sound of to his right in the area Nileen had went, like a wet fish smacked the ground to flop around. Or a body.

In his peripheral vision he saw Nileen dragging Dmytro away, through the mass of sombra that parted before the boulder of her resilience. They had their eyes on the new unclaimed prize. With a deft toss of her hand, Nileen threw something at him—hitting him in the chest and tumbling to the ground. A little white stone that glowed a soft shade of green.

HUMANS ARE PESKY LITTLE THINGS, words breathed, sounding like the howling of wind. YOUR LIFE ENERGY SO SMALL.

LIKE ANTS, SWARMING.

SQUASH ONE AND THEN MORE WILL FOLLOW.

JUST LIKE THE ATHAIANS.

HOW SIMILAR BUT OH HOW DIFFERENT YOU ARE.

WEAKER.

"It's what we humans do. Pesky little things that we are." He reached down and picked up the little stone. Irregularly shaped, the size of a marble. Its glow shined in his hand like a little cup of moonlight rimmed with a green halo.

It's beautiful…

The wraith transmogrified, the smoke surrounding it as

it pulled the body of Gleb into it. Dozens of tentacles reached up into the air, swirling and writhing together as if caught in an underwater current. Then they retreated, and the smoke dissipated once more. A man walked out from the smoke. Gleb.

"A new body? You differ greatly from the others. What are you?"

A growling sound erupted from the horde of sombra behind him as one creature made a jump for the dead body, a tentacle shot out from Gleb and repelled the sombra back towards the line of the other mass of dark figures. The repelled sombra bled back into the mass of darkness,

I saw this earlier, he thought. They're like smoke.

"Your kind will learn." The red eyes turned away from the crowd of growing sombra and turned onto Tsuske. "I'm afraid it is too late for you, though. I truly hate killing needlessly. It only makes the horde grow."

"What do you think you'll do with me?"

Gleb chuckled, a warm, hearty, human sound. "I will feed you to the horde. Your body is tantalizing to them. Perhaps you will find your family in the realm of reflections with the other unclaimed. There are so many there."

Smoke crept down the walls of the tunnel, extinguishing the lanterns one by one. One of the sombra had succeeded and had reached the dead body on the ground left by Nileen in her rescue of Dmytro, its smoky appendages still struggling down into the gullet of the body.

"It looks like you are the only one to fill their growing

appetite. Don't worry, you won't be alone in the world of reflections. If you cannot find your family—your friends will follow shortly." As the ambience of the room grew dim, Tsuske saw dozens of red eyes of the sombra turn onto him. Then the midnight figures dashed forward.

———

THE MIDNIGHT FIGURES DASHED FORWARD, charging him. The soulless standing in the middle of the room, watching the events unfold, a rictus of a smile revealing large pointy teeth as it anticipated his death.

Sombra do not attack the living!

He flung himself backwards, towards the wagons, and felt ice upon his flesh as a sombra's claws touched him before he yanked away. The cage wiggled, the thing inside squirmed within the confines. It was useless now. There were no people down here to attack save for him. And he did not want to release it and have it attack him. No point in releasing it now. He resisted the urge to throw the cage at the undead.

IT IS POINTLESS.

Tsuske looked at Gleb, the wraith. He had not spoken out loud. No, this monster was inside his mind.

"Get out of my head!"

THIS IS MY REALM. THE SUBCONCIOUS HAS ALWAYS BEEN MINE.

"My thoughts are my own. Do not try to turn my thoughts. I know what you are about now, and I know how to stop it!"

WRONG.

"You are not human. Our minds can be a powerful thing and one that we can control. You don't understand us."

DON'T I? YOU KILL. YOU MURDER... YOU IMPRISON THE INNOCENT. WE ARE THE SAME.

His back hit the wagon as the mass of darkness encircled him, hissing and moaning. I have never seen so many sombra here in the Grotto. Laughter filled his mind. The soulless rose from the ground in the body recently slain. It's head barely attached to the body; black strands of sinew made up of the creature's essence tried to hold the two together. Eyes glowing red.

AND THERE WILL BE MORE LIKE HIM.

He ignored the wraith. One of the sombra came at him from the side. He stepped up to the darkness. In front of him—a shovel meant to load deposits into the wagon lay up against the wooden planks, grabbing it he shoved back at the darkness. Pushing it back. The essence that made up his body dissipated like smoke around the shovel and it sank towards him, arms reaching for him with the husky moan of...hope? No that could not be it. Expectation. A need for mortal flesh. His body.

To kill him. To become him. They all wanted to become something. To live. To become like the slain Gleb.

Tsuske seized its shoulders as the creature grabbed him, connecting with solid form, and he shoved it away, pulling on its arm and spinning it away. It only had gone a couple feet before its head turned all the way around, a gaping hole in its face. Filling the lines were rows of spiny teeth, violet smoke escaping with a hiss. He realized that it was preparing to go inside him.

I am not even dead!

Another of the sombra came at him from his left. The features were off—the nose too big, one red eye a little higher than the other, and its face began to split in half, going up its forehead and down the back. Tentacles, smoky tendrils wiggling forth from the opening and extending towards him very much like an anemone, the gaping bouche exposed—something he had never seen before, as the sombra leaned towards him.

What the hell is that thing?

The cage rattled on his back.

Abruptly the sombra dropped to the floor, shying away from him. An opening in the line as the other sombra shied away from him. This was the moment to flee. He unslung the pack from his back and dropped the cage without ceremony and made for the break, but then the shadow folded in around him. Dark figures were all around him. Icy, cold claws groping at his flesh, cool tentacles like the touch of death itself, wrapping around his limbs, making him gasp in shock. He dropped the shovel and a dark hand grabbed that too. The body of Rotz appeared in front of him, tendrils of darkness oozing out from the gaping neck. The shovel raised high above him.

YOUR FRIENDS ARE NEXT, the voice promised. Laughter echoing inside his head.

A glowing, terrifying force hit him on the side. A horrible, mournful cry sounded inside the chamber. A medium size mass of green and purple tentacles writhed on top of one of the sombra—not on top of the soulless—the opening to its carnivorous pit sucking at the weak spot. The neck. Tentacles wrapped around the soulless in a parasitic embrace as the undead's own tentacles sprawled out onto the ground, grappling at the floor of the mine. The hole in the neck widened, being ripped open by the suction of the plant. The head fell from the body.

Utter chaos exploded in the vast chamber of the mines.

The sombra fled from the scene, moaning and inching away from the scene before them, shying to the sides of the chamber, some disappearing through the walls and vanishing into the ground. He had the feeling that the wraith could have swept him away at will. Why was it letting one of its own be destroyed by a... a plant?

Tsuske stared in utter amazement as the carnivorous plant sucked away the life force of the soulless, its tentacles beginning to glow a menacing violet color as the last remnants of smoke dissipated and was gone. It seemed to grow in size as it consumed the undead daemon. Pulsing and radiating power with each undead it took.

He had the feeling that that sombra devoured by this plant would be gone forever. Each of its tentacles made a wet mucking sound as it felt across the ground, searching for more. Searching. It turned; its bulbous head being supported by the pile of wiggling tentacles beneath its body. Small scarlet petals shun around the plants ahead.

That's not supposed to happen.

YOU HAVE WOKEN AN ANCIENT ENEMY, HUMAN,

HAVING NO IDEA WHAT YOU HAVE RELEASED UPON THE WORLD.

The cackle of laughter filled the vast mines. Tsuske turned to see that Gleb—no—the wraith had materialized and was staring at the plant in fascination. It was happy to see it. The daemon's hands were out before the creature with veneration.

The bundle of wet tentacles lurched forward, towards the shadowy wraith, its gaping maw opening to suck the life of the spirit it was seeking, but the wraith spun, an icy wind filled the chamber before it turned to smoke and vanished deeper into the mines.

Stopping its movement, the tentacle prodding the ground, searching for the entity that had just been. The antennae on its head bobbing as its head danced around searching for sombra. The sombra had formed again from the blackness. This time they did not seem to be under the influence of the wraith. They moved sluggishly, without vitality, as they moaned their woe. The plant found a sombra. Its cries did not seem to alarm the others in the chamber. These were the sombra he was familiar with. No longer bearing a semblance of humanity. No longer reacting with a thought outside of searching for a host.

Oh light, he thought, as he watched the plant devour the undead daemons. What is that thing? He stared up with alarm at the growing plant form.

The pulsing darkness had evaporated, gone with the wraith and with it the rest of the strange sombra. The image of the plant devouring the spirits, the scene a horrifying fright before him. He stepped back, behind the wagon, and quietly left the mines. The sounds of tentacles moving across the ground accompanied by the wet sucking noise filled his ears as he strode forward, arm at his side. The gun could not provide protection against sombra, but it might against a living thing. A plant that could not feel. A plant with an appetite for the dead.

19

TSUSKE

Mission accomplished.
          Sort of...

In his pocket was an artifact that could be of some use. And they had retrieved Dmytro, for which Nileen was thrilled and he was too. He was alive.

Dmytro was alive.

Tsuske was supposed to have headed directly towards the judgement room after the assignment. He felt dead tired, though his mind hummed with a new vitality. One that he knew would be swept away with the tide after the meeting with the lord emperor. He had a feeling, something about the way the guards stared at him, weighing and judging him, that everything was about to change. Axiomatic as that was, he hoped that he would have the chance to speak with her. She knew things that he did not. Things about him. About the Higaziit. Things that she should not know.

And I need answers.

The Athaian's capture sparked something in the imperials. Greed and jealousy slewed off of the echelons and out into the lower ranks of the Imperial Guard. Something had been decided while Tsuske and his team had been away on assignment. Tsuske had once been analytical about his position as Second, quiet and astute. He had not been required to think about others. His main priority had been the maintain the reliability of secured borders and safety of the empire, and to ensure the affluence of the empire remained in the hands of their ruler.

Nileen and Dmytro were off filing their reports of the incident and were not required to return to the judgement room with him. He would visit with them afterwards to relay news of the intrigue. They had promised him they would visit Director Voren and Tsuske knew that the director would endure their company; awaiting eagerly return to work. He would have many questions. Questions Tsuske may not have the answer to.

He could hear the director's voice in his mind as clearly as if he stood by his side. How well did you do tonight, boy? He wondered. You've been in charge for the last few missions. Do you understand it all now?

Tsuske thought he did. Yet—he had to see the Athaian first. He had to make sure.

Hanging over him was a giant shadow of doubt. What did she know about his family's demise? And more importantly, what did she know about the Higaziit and the Shadow King's return? Who was the Shadow King? He would have to voice it during the meeting. It was his duty.

But finding out first for himself would only benefit them all. Tying loose strings.

At the entry to the research facility, he found more guards—not the common security staff, no, these were soldiers. The lord emperor wanted this place well-guarded; not fearing the enemy whose will was against the empire's but fearing what lay within its own walls. Within its own cells. A mother and a child. The last of her kind. An Athaian. Someone dangerous.

The front of the cell block—where the detained prisoners used for experimentation were held—faced south, towards the main laboratory facility. Easy access for all the research personnel for the studies they conducted. It was here where Tsuske found the number of guards standing along the hall that led to the cells. Almost a dozen soldiers were in the hallway, outside of the cell block. He knew the people feared the Athaians, but this seemed excessive. She was just a woman with a baby.

They watched him suspiciously as he passed.

Tsuske almost stopped to inquiry them if anything had happened. But he moved on. Talking to these brutes would garner nothing more than a headache. Ten soldiers lined the walls, and they didn't challenge him. Several raised hands as if to do so—he saw from the corner of his eye—but they backed down into silence. He entered the large white hallway; two dark clad figures in refine dark green suits guarded the door up ahead.

His footsteps echoing softly down into the corridor, the attention of his fellow COBRA were on him. Finally, one called out to him as he neared. "Tsuske, sir?"

"Hello, Katana. Sniper."

Katana moved away from the wall, while his partner leaned against it, looking bored. Tsuske smiled at the pair of snakes.

"Is everything ok, sir?"

"I came to check on her," he said simply.

"What about the mission? There has been talk that it was a make it or break it situation."

"We are yet to see the results for the assignment."

Sniper looked up from his relaxed pose against the wall —an erroneous position to convey disinterest, giving him the cover to observe without looking interested—and said, "Why are you here, then? As you can see, we are watching the Ancient just fine. Or do you not trust us?"

"Of course, he trusts us, Snipes." Katana folded his arms across his chest, conviction in his voice. "We're COBRA. Brethren." He nodded at Tsuske. He didn't need confirmation, Katana believed in him, believed in what he stood for.

Tsuske met Sniper's eyes and gave him a curt nod. "I trust you both as much as I trust all of COBRA."

"Except the paper pusher turned into a rat."

"Snake food for later. She'll get what she gets." Sniper said.

"None of that," Tsuske said with a sharp gesture. "Ignore her ploys, they're just a girl's fancy to get noticed. She has lost her family. We all grieve in our own way."

"Phaw!" Sniper groaned, his mouth thinning to a line. "That doesn't answer why you are here, Tsuske."

"I want to speak to the Athaian. I need to see her."

Katana looked uncomfortable. Sniper pushed away from the wall, looking him up and down. Then he shook his head. "We were told not to let anyone in there unless they bear a special form of I.D to admit them further. I'm sorry Tsuske, but without Director Voren here—"

"Hush Snipes," Katana said. "Look at him. He has come all this way in lieu of meeting with the lord emperor. He's still wet from the night's rain. Something presses him to do this and face death in doing so. To see her again. Isn't that right, Tsuske?"

Sniper looked anything but convinced.

On any other night he would commend Sniper's will to obey, but he was beginning to feel annoyed at the delay. Every second mattered.

"See?" Katana said. "I think... I think I didn't see him down here. Actually, I haven't seen him at all today. Maybe later, when he convenes a meeting to convey to us the turn of events. And to tell us how the director is doing, too. Then—then I may see him." He turned and look down the opposite end of the cell block, folding his arms over his chest.

"But..." Sniper's mouth pinched into a small frown and then he let out a breath. "I don't see anything, either." He turned in the same direction as Katana. Adamant to not see a thing.

"That's unnecessary, I will convey my trespassing when I go and make my report."

"Do you hear something, Snipes?" Katana asked.

"Yeah," Sniper said. "Only your ugly voice."

Tsuske chuckled and took a step towards the door. He

peered through the observation window. All the cells on this block had observation windows and audio comm unit to convey speech. The room was dark, light would not be turned on until morning as the specimens would be on a strict light and dark scheduled cycle. And yet there was a manual override switch he put his fingers to, lighting the room within. He wondered how Katana and Sniper thought they could pretend ignorance of his trespassing when there were security orbs.

Something to worry about another time...

Then his eyes fell on her.

A body lay on a small cot, juxtaposition against the wall; long silvery white hair inches from touching the ground as it hung down from the bed in a messy loose plait. Another, smaller bed, three feet off the ground in a sort of cabinet, was a transparent bassinet. It was empty. Tsuske narrowed his eyes, searching. The woman on the bed moved, her socked feet pulled up tight against her body, protectively.

Have they taken her child from her already? He wondered. No, that would not make sense for why a bassinet meant for a newborn was inside the room. So where is the baby?

The Athaian's head moved, and she rolled to her back. Tsuske observed a bundle of pink flesh laying cuddled to her left breast. Then his heart quickened. Something touched his soul. A beckoning drawing him to meet her eyes. Icy blue pearls pierced through the glass window and stared at him. Lady Shivana was awake.

The door slid open, and he walked inside. A whisper, subtle and gentle on his mind said, how is it she stays in this place? She can escape if she wanted to. She is an Athaian. A gentle breeze seemed to push him further into the room. His feet moved on their own accord. Light—this was Lady Shivana. Suddenly his mind went blank and he could not remember why he had come.

She sat up, pale flesh exposed to him as she gently removed the baby from her teat and placed the child onto the bed. A content coo came from the baby. It too had a mane of white gossamer that flared around the child's head in soft curls.

The door slid closed behind him.

"Tsuske?" Her voice, melodious and spellbinding. "Why have you come to me?"

He bent at the waist in deference, his voice croaked as if from lack of use. "Hello, Lady Shivana." Words started falling from his mouth, tumbling on their own accord. "I had to see you. I don't know why, but I suspect that you know what happened to my parents. Only you know the truth about my people. I think you understand me more than anyone else. And you know about the wraith." Gasping for breath, he breathed in as the last word was squeezed from him.

She looked at him, a small 'V' forming between her eyebrows. "Why do you call me lady still? I am not a lady."

"An honorific most suited for your ladyship. For you are the last hope for this world. For humanity. And for me."

The words poured out of him. She was so beautiful. Silky waves tumbled around her face from her loose braid. She was lithe and long, slender legged, with an athletic build even after childbirth, so different from the curvaceous Gestahlian women whom often were much shorter than the men. She was as tall as a man. Though he was not considered great of height, she could easily look him in the eyes as she stood to her feet.

"You may rise, Tsuske. I am no monarch demanding such respect. I am, after all, your captive, remember?"

His tongue wanted to shrivel up in shame. "I have had guilt since taking you from your cottage." Tension was alleviated as those words poured out. He knew them to be true. He had suffered greatly since meeting this woman, and he knew that it would only grow worse. "Please, release me from your binding and let us speak frankly."

"Oh?" A beautiful smile twanged at the corner of her mouth, threatening to become full and wide with mirth. "I did not expect you to know what I did to you and your teammates."

"My—my team? Please release us and I will make sure you do not suffer. I will make sure the babe does not suffer. You have my word."

"I have already taken that breath from you. You already pledged yourself to my child's life. Do you not remember?"

He did. He had only just remembered. His mouth went dry. How am I going to keep that promise, he thought? I have a duty to the empire. And now I have a duty to the child. And the mother.

"No, I will not take a vow for my protection, Tsuske. It interferes with what the Fayth and the will of the goddess have ordained."

He felt his mind come back into control; his mouth was his own again. Questions, he had questions. What had they been? "What is the Fayth?" That was not one of the questions he needed answers for, but it had been the one at the fore point.

"The Fayth are those of my people who are in a perpetual cycle of rebirth; to serve as prism guardians, to always keep and protect the fires of chaos of all three worlds from the corrupted ones."

"I—I have never heard of this. Why have the monks not sung of it?"

"There is corruption. Look afar, Tsuske, see with open eyes. Corruption is everywhere. You must remove the corruption in order for the monks to sing true. To let the people hear the songs of the Fayth, the shadow must be pushed back. Though, I fear it to be too late."

"How many are of the Fayth and what do you know of the shadow king?" Did he truly want to know this? He wasn't sure, but he knew that he needed answers.

"There were thirteen," Lady Shivana said, sadly. "I do not know if others will be reborn. My child and I are the last of my people. The Fayth are those of Athaian blood. I am not of the Fayth. I have Athaian blood, but alas I was not chosen. Little Rose—who is to say? There should have been more. Others to guide the reborn. I fear that she will not be enough. It is too much for only one to accomplish."

"What of the shadow king? Who and what is he?"

A frown tugged at the corner of her mouth. "The Shadow King. He is one you should stay far, far away from, Tsuske. He is one of the undead. The sombra. The Hada. Though, he is not of their design. He... is the corrupted one. Born of the corruption, he is the entity's face."

"How do we get rid of it? The Sombra are all acting weird because of this shadow king. They're getting aggressive. How do we fix it?"

"You cannot. He is the lord of the realm of reflections. You cannot harm him. He is untouchable."

"Realm of Reflections?" His memory recalled hearing that from somewhere. The books from the cottage. "What can you tell me about it? What can you tell me about the realm?"

Lady Shivana shook her head, sadly. "You must go, now, Tsuske. For they come for you. They are looking for you."

"Looking? Who's looking? Damn you, woman, you changed me. The least you can do is give me answers!"

She looked at him, a baleful pity cast at him. "You must go before you are seen here. Tell not what I have told you less it be used for the shadows will."

"Why? Damn you, why can't you tell me more?"

A soft cry emanated from the sheets on the bed. "She is awake, and those vile people will come soon. I fear that it is too late for you to flee unseen." She sat back on the cot, her hand resting atop of the newborn. The baby quieted. She turned back at him, looking thoughtful. "Whatever you have brought with you, keep for now. There will be a time that it will be returned to us. Please, leave us now. Let me cherish my existence with my child for the time that we have together."

"What is the reckoning?"

"The what?" Lady Shivana turned to him, a look of concern on her face. "What did you say?"

"What is the reckoning? The shadow king said that. What is it?"

A forlorn look came across her features as she stared at the wall, her eyes distant. "You cannot stop it, Tsuske. No one can stop it from coming."

The sliding door opened and a woman he had not seen before entered. Tall with a stern face, eyes the color of the sky—not as light as the Athaian's but a color not seen in the east—and long brown hair. When her face met his, anger blossomed behind those strange eyes.

"Who are you? Why are you disturbing the Ancients rest? Can't you see that she has recently had a baby? I should have known that putting a snake in charge would only give complications."

"Hello, ma'am. I am Second in command of COBRA and I was just going."

The woman stood in his way; her eyes narrowed. "Why did you come here?"

"To check on me, Sierra. He was the one to bring me in. Don't worry about him, he is too busy to get in your way. As I told him and will say it again, I am fine. The baby is fine."

Tsuske looked at Lady Shivana and back at the woman in the white lab gown, Sierra. He decided he didn't like her. Didn't like her and the knowing frown she gave him.

"To check on you?" Sierra's eyes glanced at the Athaian before returning to his. "Well, as you can see, she is fine. The baby is fine. I suggest that you do not come back unless you have the right certification to justify the visit."

"I'll keep your suggestion under consideration. I am

COBRA." Tsuske brushed past her and left the room. The door sliding quietly behind him.

Immediately, Sniper and Katana were at his side.

"I'm sorry, Tsuske. Somehow, that scientist knew that someone had entered the cell. They must have someone monitoring the security orbs. Usually, they do not."

"This woman is important. It would make sense that they have people monitoring the orbs."

"Are you heading to the meeting?" Sniper asked.

Tsuske hesitated. He turned away from the security orb and looked back at the pair of snakes. He didn't respond immediately. The words of Lady Shivana were sinking in. "I'll be going now," he told them.

There was nothing that any of them could do to stop what was coming. Then it hit him as he made his way to the dark tower of the judgement room. He had forgotten to get answers about his family and the Higaziit.

20

TSUSKE

Tsuske stared out of the glass elevator as he rose higher in the sky. Down below he could just make out the sentry bot patrolling the grounds. Little red dots moved, white lights occasionally shining on an object. The world was asleep, but the city was awake. The citizens in their decadence would celebrate the new year for the rest of the week. One of the many celebrations that the empire endorsed.

The translucent platform slowed, and the doors opened. Tsuske stepped out into opulence. Several tall marble fire places lined the walls; diamond chandeliers hung from the three story domed ceiling. Colorful tapestries added to the intricate dark patterned smalt-glass mosaic flooring throughout; giving a grandeur attribute. The stoves were lit; makra power fueled the heat from the fireplaces. The flames that licked and danced endlessly from a spout of crystal logs.

Large doorways fit for men much taller than the average man, lead into other parts of the Imperial sky manner, no doubt leading to nothing less than grand. His feet took him to the corridor that would lead to the foreboding room that would decide his fate.

His eyes immediately locked onto the imperial soldier's that stood at attention to every doorway. More and more soldiers were replacing regular security. That bode ill. Something indeed had changed since his missions down in the cities. The soldiers gave him no more attention, their eyes roamed over him as he passed, determining that he was not a threat. He knew his way around these parts; the hallways were familiar to him as would an everyday route through town would be to the average employed worker.

Walls changed from porcelain white to a stone slab. Brightness of the large domed room faded into ambient light as he entered the tunnel. It's as if I am already walking towards the dungeons, he thought.

Torches sat in little alcoves along the stone walls. They were lit. Hot fires burning from the braziers. A sign for all to see that judgement had been past. His feet touched the red carpet, dark with age and remunerated by the convicted and innocent. Dark tapestries had hung down, concealing the openings to the windows on that wall. A cool wind blew through one tapestry, giving the hallway a cool wintry feeling. A torch flame flickered, threatening to extinguish, but it held on and continued to blaze.

They can't go out, Tsuske thought. They're infused with the stone rings of fire.

Rows and rows of soldiers lined the hallway. These stared at him as if he were the criminal. Their hands were tense on their spears. He could easily dispatch every single one of them with his handgun.

Several portraits hung between each of these soldiers; they were extravagant and cruel, giving an inlay what might become of him. Heads of gargoyles depicted with anger, pleasure and woe. Stone doors awaited at the end of the long hall. An unease filled his stomach, his legs weighed down by invisible weights. Each footstep took him closer to that waiting doom.

Two emerald eyes sparkled in the ambient firelight on the stone doors. Tiny white teeth bared open, with an elongated tongue; pressing the lever to enter the chamber. There were no guards protecting the door this time. Strange, he thought. Tsuske glanced back down the long dim corridor and saw that the soldiers were watching, eyes lit by the torches set on him.

He ran his hand through his sleek queue before his hand fell to his tie. All was in place, but a man could never be too certain that he was the image of proper decorum unless he made sure that he appeared just that. With those preparations out of the way, with all his dignity, he clasped the dragon's tongue and pushed the door ajar.

CREEEEEEEEK.

The grating sound of a stone jab sliding against another. The door opened, slowly.

A roar of laugher accosted him as he stepped through the threshold and into the large oval room. Hot air from the two lit fireplaces smacked him in the head, bringing immediate fresh beads of sweat onto his skin. The laughter died as the door closed automatically behind him. The sound of stone on stone resonated until the door was back into place. Both doors could be opened at a time, both inward and outward, but that would only occur when the guillotine was brought in with accompanied soldiers to assist in the task.

The Judgement room was large and imposing. At the end of the room was a dais, raised well above the floor sat the lord emperor, below him a few of his select elite waited. He was always seen as the one above others, whether figuratively or literally.

Like the times before, eyes scrutinized him from head to toe as he entered the room alone. Sentries against the wall, soldier's in black armored suits and fine leathers stared at him. Imperial eyes from the dais and the surrounding seats stared at him.

Tsuske came forward. He knelt before the lord emperor; head bowed low. The lord emperor immediately signaled with a twitch of his fingers for him to rise. He blinked in surprise. I am not on judgement? He wondered as he rose from the deferential position. If he had been he would have been made to remain where he had knelt.

His eyes caught the twitch of the fingers, signaling to him to take his position. Emerald eyes glinted with amusement. His suspicions told him that his uncle, the lord emperor, knew that Tsuske would have wondered at this but he would not deign to answer his fallen nephew.

He retreated to the seats where the COBRA would be

seated. His eyes widened as he saw a familiar figure. His eyes locked onto the man, shocked.

But how? Tsuske wondered.

There he was. Director Voren stood leaning carelessly onto an empty mahogany desk. A mechanical leg jutting out precariously in front of him, providing a full display of his new manifestation. It glowed with a faint trace of blue-green light. The room was quiet in his ears; the lights dimming as the center of his world shun in front of him. At the man before him.

"You're shocked to see him already moving," the brooding voice of the emperor said into the quieted room. "As were we all when he decided to finally come and report this evening. I, for one, believed he would need at least another few days before he became mobile. He was barely unconscious on my floor a few hours ago." He looked down at Tsuske and Tsuske returned the look. Green eyes of the imperial line met his black Higaziit eyes. He was the first to break that gaze as he returned his eyes to Director Voren.

The man had a coy smile on his face, arms crossed as if he had won the bet of a great game. "Nice of you to finally join us Tsuske," Director Voren said. His smile faded as he gave him a speculative look over. "Though why you dressed while you showered is beyond comprehension." This sparked a few chuckles from the men gathered in the room. Even Tsuske suffered a courtesy chuckle of his own. He had forgotten how wet he had been out in the rain tonight, and in his hurry to speak with the Athaian he had forgotten to change into something fresh.

"It is a long story." Heat rose to his face; he wasn't sure if it was from the lit fire places or embarrassment.

"Oh?" Director Voren said with an amused smile. Tsuske caught his eye and realized that something was off about the director. His eyes roved over the older man, searching him over. He looked solid. Like the man that he knew except for a leg made of steel and wires and crossing over actual flesh that too glowed a faint color where it attached to the mechanical limbs.

"He was telling us his report before you came in here, Second in Command, Tsuske," the emperor said. "Though it felt more like a story out of some whimsical girl's fancy instead of a report of actual events having taken place." This brought on another series of laughter from the men gathered, even a few honor guards chuckled though when Tsuske glance in their direction, none seemed to have moved at all.

"Oh, not that bad. More like a boy's flare for the dramatics," Director Voren said, the wry smile back on his face.

"Director Voren," a voice Tsuske was not used to hearing, spoke up from the gathered men. "You will have me out of a job if you maintain that foolish countenance." He turned to see who had spoken, and none of the faces staring back at him were that of the voice. He turned to look back at Director Voren when a man appeared off to his side, swirling amber liquid in a small glass.

The man from earlier… where had he seen him before? His mind felt numb with exhaustion.

"My new Chancellor," the emperor said from upon his dais. "Tsuske you remember him from last time, don't you?"

Tsuske looked at the older man and vaguely he remembered the man from last night. An older man, tending a tavern—the same man who had spoken up during the meeting the night before. Tsuske nodded his head.

Director Voren frowned at the Chancellor and returned his gaze back to the Lord Emperor, dismissing him. The emperor had risen and came down to the floor to retrieve ale at the small bar—waving away assistants who flanked him. "I can retrieve something for myself." Like beaten dogs, they retreated to where they would be invisible to those more important than maids.

"I think this is my first time seeing you leave your chair, my lord emperor." The Chancellor cooed into his drink. "I was wondering if that bulk of yours had been artificially placed there—alas, I am wrong. You do move sometimes."

The lord emperor chuckled as he raised his glass of amber liquid to his mouth. "If you wish to see how I've gained these muscles, accompany me to the practice yard. General Gustaav and I will show you how to become a man."

"A man, you say? I take it that I will have to wear all that armor and develop big grotesque flesh of muscle and sinew? Ah—I appreciate the invite, my lord," and with this the chancellor bowed his head with sincerity, "but I do so love my robes and gowns.

On feet too quiet to be normal, red, black and silver flourished as the older man sat back at his seat upon the dais. "Please continue, Voren, so your Second can learn of your escape from the medical wing. You were concerned for him and your team, weren't you?"

"Escape?" Tsuske eyed the Director indecisively. He found that the Chancellor had pushed a glass of the same amber stuff into his hands.

"You look cold." He said pushing the stuff into his hands. Tsuske tried to offer words of thanks but found that the man was already retreating to the mantle of the fireplace to his spot on the edge near the fire.

"After spending hours in the hospital after the surgery, I knew I needed to be out of there. Hour of trying my patience during the recovery, well, lets just say I needed out. With respect for the medics and healers, I decided that I could move around on my own. They do not really care about my health, truly. They have rules in place for patients after the surgery. If they can shit and piss without being unmanned, then they're fit to be unmonitored." He said. Tsuske could sense the humor in him, the same usual countenance he had for the world, but he also sensed that he believed in what he said, too. "As you can see, I am quite manned." This brought a few more chuckles to the room.

"That is not quite true, Director Voren." A voice from the back spoke up. It was an old withered voice.

Immediately someone guffawed, and Tsuske saw that it was General Gustaav; spewing liquor down his front like a baby without his bib at his uncontrolled mirth. His other uncle was uncouth.

The old, wiry voice who spoke, spoke a tone louder over the laughter. "We want to be sure that the sight of injury is well on the process of healing and that no infection settles in, which can happen after such a horrendous and trying procedure. Plus, you had not one, but two synthetic limbs attached to your body. You were supposed to stay in our care yesterday evening, but you had left, and we had to postpone everything while we searched for you. Why no one told us where you were... We have to be sure that your body continues to accept—"

Director Voren cleared his voice loudly, cutting the older man off mid speech and silencing the sounds of laughter that had chittered amongst the echelons present. With complete certitude he said, "Doctor Axel, I am telling my dramatic tale of recovery from a life and death injury. Unless you want to become a bard, let me finish." His words were not unkind, but it adroitly silenced the older man.

"Doctor's flocked around me to perform this relatively new form of surgery on my body as I began to die from the stresses of ascertaining such horrendous injuries upon my person," the Director Voren said with a flourish of his hands. "The operation was a success, as you all can see, but I nearly died last night. With a new prototype installed where half of my leg and foot used to be and an entirely new arm—they had to replace part of my shoulder to install the blasted thing. A prosthetic mobile robotic leg and arm. I am the first living android this empire has ever seen. I can almost feel it as I run my hand along the steel. It moves completely to my will and unconscious thoughts." He broke off from his speech, took the glass right out of Tsuske's hands and downed the drink. With a loud clink, he slammed the glass onto the dark wood next to several more emptied glasses. "I feel more alive than ever."

Director Voren stared at him, and a child ran up Tsuske's spine.

That was when Tsuske realized that the director's eyes glowed a chilling blue.

21

TSUSKE

The fires of the hearth warmed the room. Tsuske found a seat near the hearth near the new Chancellor, taking off his cloak and coat and adjusting the cuffs and collar of his shirt before settling onto the stone mantle. During these meeting, if no judgement would be past, people were allowed to shuffle and move, though most chose not to. Tsuske chose a seat near the fire, hoping they would dry his clothes, if only a little.

"Is that it?" A young man's voice filled the silence. "There has to be more story to this tale. Before your Second came in, you were telling us of a bomb going off." Tsuske looked at the man who had spoken. It was Lord Heir, Tobias. The youth was not privy to the reports they submitted to the Lord Emperor, his father. Yet he was certain that he had been well informed of the details on the assignment they had completed a few days ago. The boy was ever so interested in the COBRA.

"All the details from Agent Dmytro and Agent Nileen

are in the file. Their report came in the same day we arrived." Director Voren looked up at Tsuske, "Your file should have been dropped off then too. Where is it?" Tsuske furrowed his brow. He had yet to drop it off. Everything for the last forty hours had been a non-stop blur.

"Right here." The voice to his right spoke. The Chancellor stood up and walked to the middle of the room. He was a tall man. "I have it."

"Why do you have it, Chancellor?" Director Voren queried. Tsuske heard the breath of mistrust, though he doubted whether anyone else did.

Director Voren seemed to be the same man that I have worked with for the last five years... but why did he have glowing eyes now?

"A good question," the Chancellor said, and with a flourish he pulled out the file. He seemed to peer at it with great curiosity, before looking up and around the room as if to wonder why he garnered such notice.

"If you have it, you can tell us the details," the Lord Heir surmised, sitting back into his seat.

"Irrelevant," the Chancellor said and flurried the manuscript to the Lord Emperor. "Doctor Axel may not be a bard, but I can be. However, I think it best if you reported to us Tsuske, of your accounts of the happenings that took place that day. A tale is best heard from its source of mouth."

Tsuske narrowed his eyes. He had already reported the accounts of everything in that report.

The Lord Emperor did not reply, instead he viewed the

manuscript, flipping through the pages before his eyes settled onto Tsuske. It was evident that the Lord Emperor had already read the report. His eyes fell onto Director Voren. Those bright eyes did not provide him with answers.

Well... he had planned on discussing the matter of the assignment with the director personally, relay his concerns to the man. This meeting was not conducting as he thought it would turn out. The Lord Emperor had ordered that he receive their reports immediately, too busy with official business to see him when he and his team arrived. Accepting a documented report before omitting to see him. Dmytro and Nileen were not present in this room, so they had not been ordered to give a recounting of their reports. Tsuske looked over the room, the guards and decided it would be best to keep his eyes on the Lord Emperor as he spoke.

Why would I need to go over this again? What about tonight's mission?

He gave his formal report, again. Retelling the story. Professor Yoshi Nakamatsu seem the most enthralled by his retelling. He did not ask questions; he listened with the intentness of a raven ready for the opportunity to retrieve pickings from a wolf's kill. As his story came to the power plant and the decision to blow up the power plant, he could see horror widen the scientist's eyes before he nodded. A few others looked mortified at the recitation of his report. Particularly Doctor Axel, though his cheeks reddened as Tsuske spoke, he was not sure if from anger or something else. As he came to the departure and the malfunction of the explosives, to the injury and then their escape out via the helibird Pearl Anderson had flown in, he heard the whisper of softly spoken words discussing what he had just completed with his telling. Director Voren nodded with the retelling.

"An interesting tale," the emperor said. Tsuske could not tell if he thought his report false. His team would have written a similar account. Their reports had to be like his own. He had not had the chance to go over with them. Not that it was needed. "Director Voren, do you have anything to add to his report?"

"No," Director Voren said. "But I will submit my report sometime in the morning. It will include more details outlining the events, certainly. But nothing that would dispute Tsuske's or any of my people's reports."

"Excellent," the emperor said, and then he dismissed the entirety altogether. "Director Voren, we have heard of rumors that there has been an increase of disappearances happening in the Grotto. These disappearances are disconcerting. If enough people go missing there will be talk, and talk leads to disgruntlement."

This brought the murmurs to silence.

Director Voren and Professor Yoshi Nakamatsu locked eyes, an understanding seemed to pass between them before Director Voren spoke, "We have not requisitioned any new foundlings for some months for the science department. It has been over six months since we have brought in specimens for the medicinal wing."

The look did not go unnoticed. The Lord Emperor

turned his cold dark eyes to the head Scientists. "No new specimens?"

"There is no need. Research is progressing well. The specimens we have had garnered a substantial amount of research data. I do not foresee needing fresh specimens for quite some time." The scientist shrugged, helpless as to the cause of the most recent disappearances. "Though any drop offs of these strange sombra would be most helpful. I need them for my research. Which leaves me to ask, Tsuske, your team have no brought me what I have asked for."

Feeling eyes fall on him, Tsuske said, "No."

"Wait, we'll get to the current report soon. Answer me this. Who has been reported missing?" Director Voren asked, curious.

It was not the emperor who spoke next. Instead, he sat back on his dais and looked at General Gustaav to speak.

General Gustaav stepped forward. "Not the usual foundling or unwanted child. Those usually are given willingly at the beginning of the new year for coin. Since we have not opened those doors yet this year, we have received none unwanted child. If you have picked off any of the hooligans in the Grotto in a taciturn manner, no one has reported a missing child." He looked at Director Voren. His thoughts on the manner were dubious of that admission. He crossed his large bulky arms as he said, "No child is report missing. Instead, it is adults who have gone missing. A baker's wife. An uncle to someone employed in the military, metal workers, and a few others. These were reported to the Constabulary of Gestahl. Which thought to give me an undisclosed report of the matter."

And why would the Constabulary of Gestahl feel that it would be necessary to report to a military branch, Tsuske wondered. Instead of taking authority of this matter in their own hands, as was established for local authority. Missing people's cases were not uncommon. Reports did not garner the inspection of high-ranking members of the Empire. Let alone to be a concern for the Lord Emperor to speak of it at a private meeting with his elite.

This was unusual. But not too unusual after the evening's events that had happened down in the Grotto and down in the mines.

"That is interesting. Working force going missing is not common. Since most paid positions have an apprentice system in the guild. Journeymen and apprentices going missing is something for consideration," Director Voren said, conceding. "What have the masters of those guilds said?"

"Since not all the civilians going missing are part of a guild, we have not actually spoken with the masters of those guilds of the few who have disappeared."

"General Gustaav," Director Voren addressed. "Since you seem to want to be part of this, then tell me something. Who have you investigated?"

The large man turned to him and gave Director Voren an appraising look. He was of a height with Director Voren, but much larger in chest and arms. His sleeves of his military outfit had been torn off at the shoulders to reveal the musculature of well-worked arms—he did not dress in the imperial military fatigues as was his usual elegant attire. His chest barreled with strength. Neck and shoulder's having achieved maximum vascularity that extended down his pecks and upper limbs. Biceps twitch menacingly. His lower half of his body was just as obscenely muscled beneath military fatigues. Overall he looked clean and well dressed, as if he had not been in the practice yard this day.

General Gustaav lifted his chin. "I am starting to believe we should look inwardly before we extend ourselves to looking for a threat on the outside."

His dark eyes narrowed as he stared toward Director Voren, conveying an obvious message he thought he knew where to begin his search. To add to his words, to further outline his appeal for the idea, he said, "One would have thought the slithering snakes of the empire would have been first to hear of this news. Instead, the Constabulary had to inform me of it to get the message to us because they, the lowly Constabulary of the bottoms, noticed something amiss before the snakes did."

Interesting, Tsuske thought. For a man to be wearing training fatigues, he is not very dusty.

Director Voren was unfazed by the General Gustaav. As the director stare him eye for eye, a vein began to pulse on his uncles forehead. It did not go unnoticed by Director Voren. "That is a good thought. I believe we will have to search first with the giver of such news. Find hidden meanings and reasons that this is a cause to be upset over. What time are you available to come to my office and chat?"

"Hidden meanings and reasons?" General Gustaav exploded.

Tsuske was taken aback. The meeting had begun well, the reports given, even some amusement. Now anger?

"Look at you, Voren. Are you even a man in there, under all that metal?"

"If It's a question of my manhood, I assure you mine is still the larger, mate."

The emperor sat up on his dais, quietly observing the rising hostility between the two echelons, with an intent look on his face. He was eager for this confrontation.

"How are you still moving after surgery? You are no man, Voren. No man. You're a piece of scrap metal."

Director Voren only chuckled.

The emperor's eye seemed to soak in all the hostility radiating off his brother, the general. Was he taking pleasure between Director Voren and General Gustaav's' indifferences and hostilities? He was well known for pitting two people against each other. But his two best friends?

The emperor has no friends. He is the emperor. The thoughts came unbidden to him.

"Lazy bastards, all of you snakes." General Gustaav said, crossing his arms and taking a step back. The veins bulging in those arms, twitching insistently.

"I do not see why missing people have to concern you," Director Voren said, not taking the bait. "It is something my people can investigate, quietly. I assure you that it is most likely nothing to be upset over. Perhaps you should excuse yourself until you get your feelings under control. I hear the women's lavatories have feminine hygiene products for their monthly cycles. We can excuse you to tend to yours while we discuss this matter in a—"

"Care to say that to my face?" The larger man's arm uncurled, his fists clenched and unclenched at his waist, staring hatred at t Director Voren. Director Voren, only smile and the big man's face turned a shade darker.

"If I wanted to speak to a woman, I would go to the Velvet Bunny," Director Voren said as he stepped up to the larger man. His prosthetic leg holding him up without issue. He moved naturally and with ease. They were of a height, however, Director Voren's disposition was brought on from his years of experience and outdoor activities, whereas Director Gustaav looked like a genetically modified bull. A man of the gym and training grounds.

And perhaps artificial enhancements, if the rumors were true. Tsuske need not look into his uncles file to find the truth.

Director Voren shrugged. "People have gone missing. Not because of our own confiscations of individuals that are found violating our laws. All citizens know, young and old, what happens when you break the law. Only children six and under are given any leniencies, a first-time warning and minor punishment to ward off second offense offenders." Fire met ice as the two faced each other, noses inches apart.

A newer voice spoke up. It was the Chancellor, in a lively sort of way. "No, gentlemen. I do not think we are at fault here, nor is this a just a minor missing person case. With tonight's events, I say we have to look outside for the source of this problem before we look to each other for treason. Rest easy, you two. Drink and be merry as we discuss this. I know I shall do just so."

The Chancellor stepped up between the two men, placing a delicately manicured hand on their shoulders; each of his nails painted a different color. The emperor's eyes gleamed in anticipation for just a moment and then went dun as the two echelons backed away from the Chancellor. To take a fist to this man would be treason. Few would risk hurting such a high-ranking person, even if he had come to power only recently. Even if their own ranks were equally prestigious, striking the Chancellor would be like striking the emperor.

The Chancellor was voice of the emperor. And the emperor enjoyed employing such a man to deliver speeches and to talk in his stead.

The man who spoke was unlike anyone Tsuske had ever seen before. He had similarities to the old barkeeper in the tavern. Here, his resemblances had none of the Gestahlian identifying attributes to anyone native of the east continent of Esterine. This man was not young, nor was he quite as old as he had appeared earlier. His voice held a rustic quality that Tsuske did not expect a man of his class to have. A man just beyond his middle years, his cheeks were beardless, though he had a small moustache on his upper lip, the hairs were lighter than the color of his head; his scented and greased hair were fine and abnormally light. Not the paleness of an Athaian, and he was not as dark-haired as the emperor and his ilk, but his hair had a silky tawny quality to it. Not a brown, but not a blonde. His cheeks and forehead had been warmed to redness by the brandy he consumed. And he dressed in bizarre clothing.

Most men of prestige dressed as their trade expected

them to be. Officer's in the military were expected to dress as their men did, in military fatigues with emblems to show rank. Men in service to the empire as agents, dressed in dark green slacks and ties or the wilderness cloaks for when they ventured outside of the tower. A craftsman dressed in practical woolens of sturdy weave, colors reflecting their station and position in life. Both journeymen and novice apprentices each stood out in their trades, an insignia of rank to show the years, or lack of years, that one had to their position.

This man dressed as a nobleman. A nobleman who did not know how to match colors according to what appeased the eyes. Most nobles dressed gaudily. Not all those of nobility were of the imperial family line, some had risen to that station through luck, but all knew how to dress as if born to it. Fine tailored suites, laces and adorned with riches. And yet... the Chancellor had none of that, not where it was most easily seen. His colorful clothing mixed in their variety looked like a paletton had worked with every color he had in his warehouse to robe the Chancellor. Tsuske was never certain which station exactly the Chancellor held, but he knew it was a high one to be noticed by the Lord Emperor and to have his favors given so willingly. To hit him or abuse his person would warrant death.

There was nothing practical to how the Chancellor dressed. He gleamed in virulent greens and reds, the cloak drooped with twice the width of cloth needed to cover him so that the sides fell to the floor and he looked like a colorful green parrot with its wings dragging behind it.

The doublet that showed beneath it glowed a patent red, frilled with lavender lace at the neck and cuff of the sleeves. The collar to his outfit was twice as large as it should have been, coming well up to his ears. The inner lacings held gemstones that did not match, nor were they garish enough to garner one's wealth. They appeared oddly out of place. His leggings were a bright orange that ended below knee-length boots of earthly rich colors. His hair, not a mane or sleek back like that of noblemen, stuck up and around his head like the feathers of a ruffled bird. He appeared more like a court's jester than someone with authority.

Tsuske expected the man to pull a tall hat from behind his back and place it on his head with an adorning bird of paradise feather jutting out the back. When the man did not, Tsuske was almost disappointed.

The Chancellor was the emperor's go between man. When not on official legal tidings from the Lord Emperor, he often performed duties for others of noble bloodlines. Settling disputes, investigating the affairs of rivals, checking in on the state of affairs of the lower cities of Gestahl and act as a well-known spy when he visited the cities of the countryside of Esterine.

"I would not have given it any more thought, either." The Chancellor admitted. "People come. People go. Unless there are bodies being left for people to discover, it is hardly much to overlook." Director Voren would have shot General Gustaav a smug look if he would have been the kind of man to do so. Instead, he leaned back on the desk, propping his leg back up as the Chancellor spoke. He raised the glass to his lips and realized it was empty.

Tsuske offered the director the untouched glass that had been placed in his hands by one silent maid.

"I wouldn't mind some of that," the Chancellor said to him noticing him. Then he promptly moved to where the drinks were served. The Lord Emperor always had the stuff available for grabs. He did not want his servants here to pour for those in this chamber and expected people to serve themselves, though sometimes that did not mean a servant didnt provide drink for someone. "I mean no disrespect to the blood of those lost." The Chancellor continued when he saw Tsuske take his place near the fire, "I am the Lord Emperor's man, yet, I overlooked this detail completely."

"Are you saying you were aware of the report on the missing people?" General Gustaav asked.

"Aware of a report? No, not at all." He sipped the amber fluid intermittently as he spoke, "I was aware of the rumors, good sirs, my Lord Emperor and lord heir." He bowed as he said the last two and the Lord Emperor waived the honorifics away, bade him to continue as he saw fit. Tsuske wondered at the perceived insult of including the lord emperor and his son as an afterthought. He knew that none seemed to have noticed it, but he had. "In my past times, I am often in the company of small men, men well beneath the notice of men who sit far higher than their own station. I mingle amongst the low. Where else am I to fit in in the grand scheme of the world unless with those of my kind? I take heart, joining with the street rats and the mangy dogs of the lower cities. I hear things, the coming and going about the company of men or the lack of such company." He hesitated for a moment. "There has been talk of something lurking down there. Of Undead walking amongst the living."

"We know of this," the Lord Emperor said, tersely. Abruptly he waved at Tsuske. "Tsuske, what was your report tonight? I was told you narrowly escape with your lives, again."

"Again?" Director Voren's brow furrowed. "Tell us of what happened. I am not aware of you being on assignment."

"You were part of the meeting last night, director," tsuske said gently.

"I can't seem to recall." Director Voren's eyes roamed the room. "It's all a blur. If my Lord Emperor will permit it, I would like to hear the report."

Tsuske looked to the lord emperor. This was his moment to tell them all about what had conspired this evening. The Lord Emperor gestured at him to be on with it.

"The rumors are true. There are a lot of sombra down below. More than the reports are indicating. They come and go, so the numbers will never be accurate. Last night, what my team and I saw down in the mines was unheard of. I am still adjusting to it myself."

"More of changed sombra?" Professor Yoshi Nakamatsu said. "And what of the odd one, the one that said it was the shadow king?"

Tsuske nodded at the professor. "Yes, there were both the ordinary sombra and the odd ones. The aggressive kind. And yes, the one who calls itself the shadow king was there." He took a breath and cleared his throat for what he was about to say. "The shadow king can impersonate a person at will. I don't know if it's after he consumes the host body or at will."

"You just said it was at will, so which is it?" Professor Yoshi Nakamatsu demanded.

Tsuske resisted the urge to shrug. "Both, probably. I am not sure."

"Are you saying that it can consume multiple bodies?"

"Yes, that is what it seems like."

Professor Yoshi Nakamatsu nodded into his hands. "Then let us assume that it can only transmogrify to the bodies it has consumed. At least until proven otherwise. I would hate to assume this thing is greater than we realize."

"But it is greater than we realize," Tsuske said, the words tumbling from his mouth. "It is dangerous. It controls these sombra. At least the changed ones."

"How interesting," the professor mused.

"Yes," Tsuske agreed. "And there is more. The shadow king mentioned something about a day of reckoning coming. More of these sombra will arrive. And the plant—the visceralia, it attacked and ate the sombra. It's still down there." He let out a sigh.

The Lord Emperor looked intrigued, and then he looked at the professor. "Nakamatsu. Can the visceralia change, too? If I can recall something of these plants, they feast off of other plants and life forms. Dangerous creatures when full grown, useful when small."

"Yes, the visceralia feasts off of plants and animal life that live near makra crystals and pools. I have never seen them attack sombra before and both have been in proximity to the creatures in the labs. I would have to conduct more research. Tell me, Tsuske, why did you not bring the visceralia back with you?"

"With me, no, that would be impossible. It's far too large now to move safely." Puzzled eyes stared at him, demanding answers. "It's in the mines. It began to grow at an incredible rate as it consumed the changed and unchanged sombra."

"YOU IDIOT, you left in in the minds? How long ago was this?" General Gustaav fumed. "We will need to send incinerator squads down there right away."

The Lord Emperor stared at Professor Yoshi Nakamatsu before the professor replied. "More studies will have to be conducted. I do not have the answers for these phenomena as it is new to me. I'd like the visceralia to be retrieved, alive, if possible."

"Scientist, you are a damned fool if you think that something like that could be detained alive if it has grown." The general only shook his head.

An old decrepit man floated up to the center of the room, and voices hushed when he spoke. "Young man," the old voice of Doctor Axel spoke up. "Did you say the reckoning?"

Tsuske nodded his head. "I did."

"Oh, that is terrible news. I fear that we are about to enter a dark age, the history of the past being repeated."

"Why do you say that Doctor?" Tsuske asked. Thoughts

were running strong. He could sense Director Voren standing near him like a wall of fire. Tsuske moved away from the hearth.

"Ancient tombs long lost to us once said that the undead will rise, and the shadow king will walk once more because the guardians are all gone. The fires of chaos are unbound and imbalanced and the protectors are no longer bound to the Fayth. We cannot stop what comes."

Tsuske looked at the older man. It was as Lady Shivana had said.

22

TSUSKE

"The Fayth?" Professor Yoshi Nakamatsu said, thoughtfully. "I think I have heard that term before. What do you know of it, doctor?"

"Not much, unfortunately. I could find out at another time." The old doctor's eyebrows wiggled with thought. "There could be records located at the Bodeian Research Facility."

"It is strange," the Chancellor said. "How these hada are growing in number."

"Hada?" Doctor Axel asked, narrowing his eyes. "Usually only those of the west call them that. The people of the Grotto call them undead. Or sombra, as we refer to them as." Unlike many of the individuals in the room, he often visited the lower sections of Gestahl. He had small clinics stationed in every district. He did not need to abduct healthy children for experimental treatments. The poor often were ailed enough, and he found that they will let the

Doctor experiment with potential treatment options on their sick. Often he was successful, both in obtaining willing specimens and in the course of his work he found a viable treatment that proved effective. He had invested a lot in his work down there. When he was not working in the Imperial tower's medicinal wing, he was often down below in the company of two of his own young children as he worked.

The technology he carried around with him, or more rightly put, that carried him around, proved to be enticing for the gutter rats and hooligans, which often followed the doctor about his business. The COBRA have taken down street thugs on the prowl just by surreptitiously tailing the good doctor about his work, picking off gang members and would be criminals that took too great of notice in what did not belong to them. "Did you say, Hada?" The old doctor asked again.

"Sorry, not Hada. But Soulless—the changed ones." The Chancellor remedied.

"Soulless are not uncommon." Tsuske found himself speaking when the silence lengthened. "It is why we mandate all bodies to be burned. The General's soldiers can often be heard being called to duty into the Grotto, to ride out to where a body has risen." It was something the COBRAs also looked out for when they were lurking in the streets of the lower city.

"In the smaller towns of the districts, people often forget that there are rules in place. They forget the rules are there to protect them more than hinder them. They think that their beloved lost one differed from the others and do not deserve to be burned like the rest are burned." The Chancellor provided.

"They are often too poor to have much of a say on what they do with the dead. The Forests within the walls cannot be cut down less ye wished to earn death. People rarely have the means to burn their own, let alone pay for the Incendiaries for pick up and carcass disposal." Tsuske felt awkward at having defended the poor of the Grotto. "Soulless are not uncommon down in the Grotto. They are usually seen in one of the smaller villages or towns, having been seen usually near where there is death. The living feel sympathetic to the lost souls, usually leaving food outside their doors at night—though that does nothing for the sombra, except to attract pests."

"The corpse of a hen distilled in the blood of an ewe, offer thy stew or they come for you." Doctor Axel whispered quietly. "Ah, yes. I have heard this a few times. Sometimes, outside my clinic doors at night, I will see empty plates or bowls. Always empty. I thought people were eating outside my clinics as they waited for treatment and did not clean up after themselves. Always when I returned the next time. The bowls and plates are gone."

"Lock thy door and gutter thy lights, whisper no name in the darkness of night, the wisest man asks for no more when the shadow king comes to the door." The words came from Tsuske, spoken as if in prayer, "Thou mother, thou sister, thou child unborn; the dead do not sleep while the world is torn. Fire to burn. Ash to smother. Wind to tear. Light to blind. Ice to bind. Water to cleanse after the fires are done." The words poured from his mouth like vomit.

He did not understand what spell was placed on him to chant this nonsense out. They all stared at him. Director Voren looked up and at him as if for the first time. "I don't know where I heard that from."

"Sounds like you might have read one of the old texts," Doctor Axel said with awe. "I would like to ask you some questions later, Tsuske."

"Were you born to one of the noble houses?" The Chancellor asked.

Tsuske cleared his throat but did not look down in shame. "I had been but removed to better serve the lord emperor and the empire."

"Ah, I see. And you, director Voren. Are you, too, of the blood?"

"No," Director Voren said. "I don't need highborn blood to get where I am at."

"It's true," the Lord Emperor chuckled. "It's your mouth I so desired. Your earnestness to use it. Your loyalty. You were a lucky find when I was my son's age."

Director Voren grinned. "You've been a pain in my ass ever since."

"Literally," the Lord Emperor laughed.

Tsuske sensed something, an untold story between the two of them. A story likely never to be spoken about outside those involved. Director Voren gave him a wink and he couldn't help but feel the reprieve of having the attention diverted from him for a short time.

"Most COBRA join our ranks from one of the noble houses. Though, like myself, there are a few who join our ranks born to pond scum. Once a snake, always a snake."

"Ah, that makes sense," the Chancellor said, not sounding convinced. "Many organizations have the same ideology upon joining." He mused, and then he looked at Tsuske. "Tsuske, where had you heard that saying?"

"I don't know," he said, feeling heat rise to his cheeks.

"Ah—well, when you remember, please come and talk with me." The Chancellor eyed Tsuske again, that same curious look he had given him when he first came into the Judgement room. "I read it once before in a book, never thought to hear the words spoken aloud by anyone not of the monkhood and that tight lipped lot keep to themselves."

"What does a book have to do with any of this?" General Gustaav questioned disparagingly. "People are missing or dead. Some of my people's family's are missing. My soldier's need closure and the rest of Gestahl, regardless of whether they're low born."

Ah, so is that why the Constabulary consulted with the general, or was there something more to the story? Tsuske wondered.

Tsuske looked up at the lord emperor to see that his uncle was looking bored.

"Good question," the Chancellor said jovially, "It does not. Just coincidental to a common topic at hand."

"Nothing to do with these missing people's cases or sightings of soulless and oddly behaved sombra. The latter is hardly worth noting since it is, as the snake-boy said it, not uncommon in the Grotto for one of the dead to walk amongst them. Fed like stray dogs, they stay near their homes. Those reports can be investigated, and the cases closed with the disposal of such carcasses as is needed. The missing people have a chance to be found alive. This should be our priority, if it were up to me."

The Chancellor eyed Tsuske over the rim of his empty glass, when he noticed the glass empty a look of dismay marred his otherwise handsome features.

"The sayings are from the monks of old. There are many other verses that were once taught to the villages back in those times," Director Voren said thoughtfully. "The monks in the history books were once a people who believed in the spiritual development of every living creature. They took great part in the villages and the daily lives of townsfolk. Teaching them their letters, their numbers and a life of peace. They were living examples of what the old teachings taught." Tsuske eyed the director. He seemed to know a lot. He wondered if he had spoken to an Athaian about this topic before. It sounded something Lady Shivana knew well.

"They are just a religious group. Closed mouth and tight-lipped except to those that live amongst their fellowship," Professor Yoshi Nakamatsu said. "That group of people do not have the minds for science."

The Lord Heir scoffed before his mouth drew to a line. Eyes turned onto the heir. The attention from the court did not make him shy, instead he glanced up, his eyes scanning the crowd before they rested on the dancing flames of the fireplace. "While I was out training with the honor guard, we would see them sometimes. They kept to their monasteries and temples. I learned that they would only come to the towns in the early morning and at night, virtually when no living being was present. They weren't rude but neither did they behave deferentially when I stood in their path."

He seemed to hesitate before continuing, "Instead, they walked around me as if I was a stone and they the river bed moving past me, unseeing. I would have cut off all their heads with a guillotine I have seen in storage—the gods know we have not use that thing in a very long time, but the officer of the guard had informed me that not even my order could kill one of them. When I threaten to knife them, they told me that I could not. They said I could have them punished in return when we returned to the Capitol, and I did. And yet who are they to tell an heir what they could and could not do? What else was I supposed to have done?"

He did not seem pleased with what he had done. He looked pensive, as if he regretted having to deal out the punishment. "Just three lashings for every guard who had accompanied me that day, and then a round of drinks afterword's. Later I learned that the monks were off limits from the commands of death or punishment. Any who wronged a monk faces prison time—which means becoming possible candidates for research subjects. No guard would have risked that. Since I could not kill the skulking old men, I did the sensible thing. I approached them and asked them a question. And do you want to know what I asked?"

None dared to speak and to this the heir frowned. "I asked this this, 'Why do you avoid the public eyes when you ask those same people for contributions of food? Where had all the old songs gone to? What is it that you hide from the rest of the world? What are you afraid of?'"

The room was deathly quiet as the Lord Heir spoke. Tsuske understood that he was young but a youth who already had years of experience of life.

"You see, some of those questions might seem irrelevant. Why would I ask them about songs? Well when mother was alive—" he was caught off by a loud guttural clearing and Tobias flushed crimson. "—I mean, well, when I was younger, I had heard the songs of the monks. I missed seeing them. Missed hearing them. Their preaching is nice and dandy and all but their songs, mournful and yet holding meaning.

As you can all guess, the monks did not speak to me when I asked them these questions. I was angry but more than that, I was curious. I wanted answers. I came back in the morning, first thing, prior to the sun's rising. I asked the same question, 'Why do you avoid the world? What are you afraid of? Where had the old songs gone?'. And again, I am ignored. I dislike this. I had the guard's block off the main streets; they do not like it, but it is not physically restraining or hurting one of the religious monks. They are not eager to do it, but they do it. When the monks saw what we had done they went around it. When those are blocked, they found other ways to walk the streets, ignoring us and any who may see them. Most ignore them, I suppose we must have proven quite the spectacle and local gossip of the town. Initially, people giggled as we passed. After the first few were publicly birched for proving annoying the spectators avoided us entirely.

Several days of this approach go by and I found that I would best get my answers from one whom is in charge." He cleared his voice and took a drink of the water he had on the dark mahogany wood. "So, I go to the temple of a small district town in the lower Grotto. As the monks leave their temple to walk the town, I learn that they pray as they walk. They grow silent when people are near. But as soon as they feel that people are gone or out of earshot to any wandering ears, they speak uniformly in a sing-song chant."

"The Monk's Hymn. Often called the Hymn of Two Halves," Director Voren said with consternation.

"I have heard of it," Tsuske said.

"Two Halves?" The Lord Heir asked and then, "Wait, you have heard it, too? When?"

"Two Halves refers to the Fayth and the Goddess," Doctor Axel said.

Director Voren nodded towards Doctor Axel in appreciation and then said, "Our job allows us to hear things when others think otherwise."

"They're snakes, Lord Heir. You cannot expect anything respectable from them," General Gustaav said darkly.

The Lord Heir, with youthful optimism shining in his eyes, shook his head. "No, that is not true. I respect the work they do. They hear when no one else listens."

"Expect, Lord Heir. I said you cannot expect anything respectable from them." His uncle corrected, but the Lord Heir did not seem to hear him. He rose from his seat next to his father and all watched as he stepped down from the dais and came closer to Director Voren. Tsuske moved in close.

"Do you want to know what I learned from them that day, Director Voren?" He asked, eager to find someone to discuss what he learned. Before Director Voren or Tsuske could respond, he said, "I went to find the head monk. I found him; I think. He was old, ancient, and walked with a staff with a weird crystal set into it. I think he is blind, for his eyes were almost completely white and he did not seem to see me. I saw him in the middle of the temple, watching the others walk out of the gates. That was when I heard their message, or part of it before they cut off as they saw our approach. He must have heard our approach. A puzzled look on his face before he smiled at us. He said to us, to me that is, 'I have been expecting you.'" He waited for either to respond.

"Go on, son," Director Voren said.

"So, I asked him, 'How have you been expecting me, you cannot even see who I am.' He then says to me, 'That is not the question you have come to ask me.' And I tell him that it is not. I ready myself to ask my question as he seems intent on hearing my words, but when I open my mouth, I could not remember the words. The question is there, but I could not remember how to formulate the words into the question I want to ask. I fear I would only get one chance to ask this question, one question that he would directly answer me that day and I could not ask it."

General Gustaav spat out, "Sorcery!" He hit a hand into his fist with a meaty thud. "That is what monks are known for. Secrets and sorcery. Almost as bad as the Athaian ilk."

The Lord Heir nodded to that as if acquiescing but what he said next was, "the old man seemed to know my question, for he answered anyway, even though I had asked nothing. He said, 'When the world falls to darkness, where do people hide? Into the homes that give them warmth and provide them their bread and their butter. When the sun fails to go away, and the sustenance that keeps people living shrivels up from the fires, where do people hide? They do not. They go out and search for their bread and their butter and hope not to be scorched by the heat.'"

Tsuske found his mouth had fallen open at the strange words. It had a hint of a prophecy in those words and yet when he dissected the words and tried to wrap his mind around it, he could not puzzle out the meaning. Director Voren equally looked puzzled. General Gustaav was not so subtle, he guffawed a loud abdominal laugh, spittle flew from his mouth as he roared with mirth.

"As I have always said, them monks are crazy old men. Religious and not worth a bother. Their sorcery is for manipulation of words and logic to their own reasonings beyond the grasp of normal humans. I think the only reason the Lord Emperor keeps them around is because they help keep the populace in check in the old ways of servitude."

The Lord Emperor chuckled darkly at that.

The Lord Heir furrowed his brows, "There is more. I have not finished yet." Eyes returned to him and Director Gustaav stemmed his flow of mirth, though he continued to chuckle to himself as the youth spoke. "After the old man spoke, he waddled away. I still had not asked my question. The words he said almost sounded like a prophecy or an omen, or perhaps, as uncle Gustaav surmised, words from a madman. He looked back at me. My honor guard wanted to go. They dislike being in the monk's monastery. They told me the wind blows the wrong way in the temple, whatever that means.

And the old monk, looking back at me he asks, 'What is your question?' And suddenly, I know it. The words form in my mouth and flow through my lips like a song from a canary. I just knew the words, and the question seemed right, in that moment, though in retrospect I could not remember why I had asked him the question.

I asked him, 'What do the monks search for when they go on their pilgrimages?' And then he stares at me for a very long time. I think he must have forgotten my question, or that he had fallen asleep while standing up. Shaking his head, he speaks so quietly that I have to lean in close to hear his words; he says to me, 'We search for the light that may be lost if the song of the bird is not caught on the hoarfrost of the reckoning.'"

Puzzled glances all around the room. The Lord Emperor sat up straight in his chair. He looked on the verge of speaking.

"As you can see, why I am on this tangent. He mentioned the reckoning." He held up a finger to stall people from interrupting his speech when a few made to talk. "I had one other question I wanted to ask him, though I hesitated. 'What will catch this bird before the winter freeze of tomorrow?' and the old man smiles at me and sort of shrugs as if to say he does not know, but then he says, 'Perhaps a cage will catch this bird.' I feel the old man is making fun. I ask, 'Why would a cage catch a bird's song?'

And he looks at me and smiles. 'Why else does a caged bird sing when its mother wishes for it to only fly free?'"

The room fell into quiet, thoughtful silence. Tsuske couldn't help but wonder if all youth were so long-winded when delivering speeches.

"When did all of that occur?" the Lord Emperor finally asked when he was certain that his son had nothing else to say.

"I have not been there since the Autumnal Fall. I do not think I will ever see that man again. He must have been a sorcerer, or perhaps just a madman. He was not a normal monk one would expect to find. He spoke with the precedence of an omen on his tongue. My honor guard feared to return nor I have not pressed them. Neither have I wished to set foot in that temple again."

"Why have you withheld this until now?" the Lord Emperor asked.

"I feared they were words spoken by a senile old man," the lord heir admits, abashed. "But the words reckoning had me thinking. Made me remember."

"Word's from an old madman are to be taken lightly. Monks are not immune to the instabilities of old age," General Gustaav said reasonably.

Doctor Axel looked like he might want to ask a question then the voice of the lord heir spoke as if just noticing something that had been long obvious to the others; "Why are you so wet?" The youth asked with surprise as he stared at Tsuske from the dais. "I thought it was sweat from the fireplace, but when you moved away from it, I could see that you are soaked through."

"Lord Heir Tobias," the Lord Emperor said bemused. "He fulfilled his assignment instead of face death. We had his team watched, and they did what they were supposed to do, with the capabilities that they can perform."

"Oh," the Lord Heir said, not as a means of apology but for the answer to his father. He looked back at Tsuske quizzically, as if he still expected an answer.

"It was raining outside," Tsuske said, earnestly. The look the Lord Heir shot him almost had him stepping back. The boy, not quite a man, stared at him through lowered lids. Perhaps that was not the answer he had been looking for? Then he realized he had forgotten the honorific. "My apologies, Lord Heir."

The boy shrugged as if something else had been preoccupying his mind. "I just thought you would look different, is all."

Tsuske look at him, wondering what that had meant.

23

TSUSKE

He stared at the young boy who stood at his father's side, trying to emanate the regal figure that was the emperor. The youth only had a few more years before he would be considered ready to take on the role.

"Gentlemen, we are getting off track," the head scientist said. All eyes turned to him and he stepped forward. He had been one of the few who had chosen not to sit when the meeting began. He had refused all refreshment. "With tonight's occurrences during this COBRA assignment and the rumor of Soulless down in the Grotto; investigating the causation of these disturbances is more important than the missing individuals. Perhaps it is a coincidence, but it could be consequential. The mentioning of a reckoning will need to be researched further. All of this indicates that we have trying times up ahead."

"Agreed," Director Voren said. "Any rumors of Soulless takes precedence over any missing individual civilians. The new occurrence of this shadow king is very disturbing. Investigating this creature takes pertinence over all else."

"I do not see why both cannot be investigated simultaneously," General Gustaav said in his deep voice. Tsuske heard in that voice that he believed the missing individual cases were more important than dead bodies walking around, being kept animated as sombra took host of the corpse.

But why? Tsuske wondered at that. Who was missing that caught the general's attention?

"Then let them approach this as two different incidences," the Chancellor suggested. He raised each hand, "One for the missing individuals. One for the soulless shadow king. They're both pertinent to the matter at hand. That should appeal to you both."

"If the missing individuals were Upper Gestahlians, I would favor the idea," Director Voren said. "I feel that it is not something worth investigating." General Gustaav narrowed his eyes at Director Voren's words. Director Voren did not miss the look shot at him. "We do not have the manpower to investigate missing apprentices or journeymen that cannot check in with their masters."

As if knowing his words would spark a new argument between the two directors, the Lord Emperor leaned forward slightly as he spoke. "Set aside a score of your people to investigate this issue, equally." The Lord Emperor concluded. "This discussion has gone on long enough. I grow weary of these trifling matters."

"Yes, my Lord Emperor," Director Voren said with a bow. He did not seem displeased with the decision. With that matter completed, he straightened from his bow and glared challengingly at General Gustaav.

He felt an awareness on his body when he looked up, he saw green eyes shining down at him. The eyes of a predator staring at him from the floor of the dais. He confirmed it was not Director Voren those dark eyes penetrated. Lord Heir Tobias was a tall youth. When he was of age, he would be as tall as his father. He had a strong jawline, with shoulder length hair like his father's. Unlike the mane of the Lord Emperor's, the Lord Heir slicked his hair back, holding it in place with a fine grease. Shiny with glossy light as the fireplace reflected off his onyx colored hair. Like most of the aristocracy, his hair was darker than his eye color.

"Now, we can move onto other matters." The Lord Emperor began but trailed off as his eyes focused on the back of the room. It was by chance that Tsuske saw what curtailed next.

The Chancellor had neared towards the back of the room, towards the large stone doors. Tsuske first saw the man in the corner of his eyes as an array of color. When he turned to see the man pressing his ear against the stone doors, he caught the notice of the Chancellor.

As the strange man turned to see who he had attracted the notice of, a smile split across his face, and the man flourished his deep blue cape, pulling it up to the level of his eyes secretively. He pressed his ear back to the stone door, listening while keeping his eyes on Tsuske, as the room's occupants watched him.

He really does represent every color in the rainbow. His

leggings are more an apricot than a true orange. It could be mistaken for a dirty yellow...

Abruptly the Chancellor pulled back on the dragon head's interior twin, pulling open one of grating stone doors just as a figure stumbled into the room and right into the arms of the Chancellor.

A scream, high and feminine, broke out from the man's embrace. Both of the soldiers positioned in the hallway peered into the room before ducking away as they determined that nothing was amiss.

Ah—so there are guards tonight? He had wondered why they had been absent earlier.

The figure, no doubt a woman, pulled away hastily, and the man stepped back, still holding the cape up to his face. The high collar of his cloak sticking up ridiculously as he hunched and flourished the cape with malevolence.

"Who are you?" she exclaimed.

"I am me!" the Chancellor declared. With a flourish of his cloak and cape, he bowed and then rose.

"Pearl Anderson, please come in." The Lord Emperor welcomed her with a warmth in his gaze atypical to his cool dark green gleam. At her wide-eyed stare of the vibrant man, the Lord Emperor said, "I see you have yet to meet my new Chancellor."

Something indeed had changed from earlier. Last time I had seen this chit, she had earned the ire of the lord emperor. What had changed?

"New Chancellor?" Pearl asked quizzically, pulling away from the strange colorful man. She sashayed into the room, the curving gait of her walk was only slightly put off by the man at her side. "Whatever happened to the one of old?"

"He displeased me." the Lord Emperor said curtly, a small wry smile on his cruel lips.

"Ah—well, I hope this one is more to your liking." She eyed the Chancellor dubiously and then succinctly ignored him.

"We shall see," the Lord Emperor agreed. The look in his eyes was intent. Cold, calculating. Waiting. Had he forgiven her for her audacity? Tsuske did not think so, despite the girl's stepping pride.

The previous chancellor had been a much older man with terse replies, only responding to direct questions. Never conversational. Never seemed to be where anyone expected but the work was often completed when the reports were needed. He was not usually to be seen in the company of the Lord Emperor or any of his men of power. Tsuske liked the previous chancellor for his covert workings and wondered briefly what fate had befallen the old man.

Why have a chancellor around suddenly? Tsuske narrowed his eyes at the peacock of a man.

"You wish to see me? Well—so you shall see!" The Chancellor flourished both of his long-robed sleeves like a bird flapping to the appraisal of its fellows, silk lacing of every color flowed down to the connecting seams of the cloak.

He truly looked like a colorful bird that had just migrated for the spring to a den of ravens and sparrows...

When he had finished with this antic, the room fell into

silence. No one really knew how to react to such a vacuous display. The new chancellor put everyone off. "And so you saw. Spell-bound and silenced into awe."

Tsuske took in a breath of air. The lack of propriety befitted the role of Chancellor was unseemly. The lack of decorum from an ordinary person would be offensive in the eyes of nobility. The royalty were well known for taking insult on their dignity. Inanity, save for a court's jester, was a cause for contempt and overall seen as improper. Houses warred against each other for offenses half as improper as the one given just now. With a mere movement of the Lord Emperor's finger, the Chancellor would be knelt and his head made to roll free. The carpet was not red for any other reason save to hide the blood that was spilled in this chamber for the infractions against the empire.

Tsuske watched, they all did, to view the Lord Emperor's reaction. When it was obvious that nothing would happen, a few chuckled. The honor guards lining the room eyed the Chancellor as if a cat waiting for the bird to alight down before it.

Were one of them the one who took the life of the previously chancellor? Tsuske could not tell.

Pearl ignored the outlandish display and bowed the woman's form of deference before straightening, a provocative gesture given what she wore. "Lord Emperor, I apologize for my late arrival. I have come to discuss matters of great importance." Pearl Anderson took in a breath of air as if to calm the flutter of nerves. Her bosom rose and fell around the low-cut neckline of her blouse, which emphasized more than it hid.

"Be still my heart," the words whispered into the room and eyes fell onto the youth who had spoken. The Lord Heir blushed furiously, but he did not turn his eyes away.

The Chancellor mused. "I have that effect on some." The youth's cheeks reddened further. He opened his mouth to reply but grimaced and folded his face into his hands. "It is nothing to be ashamed of." The Chancellor licked his lips.

Pearl Anderson ignored the Chancellor like an annoying moth in the room that will eventually reach the flame of the torch. With her hands on her hips, she smiled at the Lord Heir. Her blouse was tucked neatly under a black high waist pin tucked pencil skirt. Her long legs burned a gleaming bronze in the firelight. Bright red stiletto heels gave her more height than she was born with. "Hello Lord Heir, Tobias. I see you there, even if you do not wish to see me." She waved a hand affably at the youth. Tsuske narrowed his eyes but tried to keep his expression neutral. Something had definitely occurred in his absence.

"I see you too, Pearl Anderson. How are you? How did your mission go?"

She smiled at the Lord Heir but did not respond, instead she looked up to the Lord Emperor and bowed at the waist again and did not rise until the Lord Emperor bayed her, "Rise, Pearl. There is no need for formality at this meeting. Not much anyway."

"Thank you, Lord Emperor," she said, deferentially.

"Answer my son's question. How did your mission go?"

"I visited the Royal Fountains in the square, there are no

protestors as the rumors suggested. Little of last night's foray has been discovered. Civilians are calm and enjoying the festivities. However, there is some discord amongst them. Not many, as one would believe. It is mainly the laborers who display such disunity. Believe it or not, some who were allowed up here to celebrate have the audacity to voice contention. Few, but enough to have been heard today. There have been rumors that some may try to enter the war bird aviary—I would suggest checking on your bird a little more often, lord heir." She blew him a kiss and in reply he turned crimson.

"Protestors?" Director Voren asked. He shot Tsuske a look and Tsuske shrugged. Intel had received no reports of an unusual dissension in the populace of Capitol Gestahl.

"It is a rather recent development," Pearl said coyly. Pleased that she had news that the snakes did not have.

Director Voren crossed his arms, "Why don't you tell us about it?"

Pearl Anderson shrugged but turned her eyes back to the Lord Emperor. The Lord Emperor waved her to continue.

"There has been strange things the people whisper about, my Lord Emperor. Talk about a Soulless taking the tramway and using the railroads in the Grotto to gain access to the upper city. That isn't the only bit of news I could curtail from the gossip. The Soulless had been seen in the company of a companion."

"The shadow king?" General Gustaav suggested.

Pearl frowned, "I don't know who that is."

"Seems like you do not know as much as you think you

do," the lord emperor said. "You can play catch up on that later."

"Yes, my lord. Though I know naught of this shadow king, I have heard that men in dark uniforms were seen with this shadow king on the tramway. I heard whispers that the people think it's the COBRA's doing, that they were escorting it up here to infiltrate the tower."

Tsuske narrowed his eyes at her. What was her game?

There had been gasps of incredulity. A Soulless being escorted to the top city by COBRA? Preposterous. General Gustaav seemed the most incensed. He punched his fist into an open palm, gesticulating towards Director Voren, who in turn glared coldly at the display.

"You filthy slimy snakes!" He growled. "How is it that none of you slithering sneaking slugs never heard of this? Because you have been in collusion with these serpentine creatures. You have eyes and ears everywhere. Why is it that this chit of a girl shows you up, Voren? Is she more of a man than you are? Where was your intel when this girl has answers that none of you have?"

Director Voren ignored the angry military man and stared at Pearl Anderson as if he had never seen her before. Or perhaps, trying to figure out how she fit into the all of this. Tsuske tried to catch his eyes, but the Director was intent on the girl. What did he know? Or suspect?

"A Soulless seen in the company of a person clothed in dark attire? How interesting." The Science Department head looked thoughtful. "If we can apprehend both the fiend and the suspect chaperoning the monster, that would be pertinent. Pending upon the details gathered from the interrogation, the data could precipitant a new scale to further understand the relationship of the living and the dead. The possibilities are most intriguing."

"Keep your morbid fascinations in the lab," General Gustaav lambasted with a growl. "Our citizens are at risk. Soulless belong in the cornfields where they originate, not in the city!"

"They belong to the dead where they ought to remain," Director Voren countered. He had not taken his eyes off Pearl when he spoke.

She took his words to mean something unsaid between the two. "I agree. There will be no phoenix amongst us." Her words prompted an immediate scowl on the director. The lord heir looked thoughtful, and the Lord Emperor looked just as pensive.

The old voice of Doctor Axel spoke up, just barely audible above the raucous outbursts from those assembled. "Perhaps we should check the video feed, see if we can catch the people who were involved. If the trams caught something amiss, then perhaps others have too. There must be someone who had seen the creature and the person accompanying it. Most likely there is more than one culprit involved."

Tsuske agreed. "This will need to be investigated. It might be something harmless. An old widow who just couldn't let her husband go, or perhaps a child with a bond to a dead dog. Before we are unsettled by this news, I think we need to investigate this more."

Director Voren nodded and turned, facing the Lord Emperor. "I agree with my Second. Now, before this derails into further discussion, I think we need to speak about why we are all gathered here this evening. This meeting has gone on long enough, and I can tell that you grow weary, my lord. If I may, Lord Emperor?"

The Lord Emperor looked at Director Voren before waving him to begin. Tsuske saw that the emperor did look fatigued by the long carried conversations that had span over an hour and a half.

Director Voren turned to Tsuske, and that is when he hesitated. "There is another reason why we are here tonight. Why, I came so soon after surgery." His hand rested on Tsuske's shoulder. "I have been makra infused."

"Makra infused? Ah—yes, I see it in your eyes. That is to be expected, you now have parts of you that need the power."

Director Voren smiled, but it did not hold any humor. "The COBRA are scheduled for the administration of this new dose starting tomorrow morning, Tsuske."

The world lurched.

"It has been in the planning stages for days, weeks actually. But, it was only approved recently, and with recent events, we need to move things forward."

Tsuske's vision dimmed, the shadows stretched along the edges. Even with the fireplaces lit in the room, his sight began to grow dark. "I don't understand what you're saying."

"The good doctor and the mad scientist decided to keep me from death. They collaborated with each other and it kept me alive. I am no longer human, Tsuske. Not entirely. But not entirely android. And it has been decided that you and the COBRA will be given similar treatment. Look at what it has done for me—what it can do for you all." He held up his mechanical arm. It glowed a light misty blue. But Tsuske didn't need to look at the director's arm to see him changed. His eyes, those startling blue eyes said it all.

"No longer a man, either," General Gustaav said.

Tsuske didn't bother to look at his uncle. He heard the words in his ears. The condemnation. No longer a man.

"I could become a full-blown cyborg, Gustaav, and I would be more man than you ever will be."

"It is true," Professor Yoshi Nakamatsu said. "I was there when this man, ahem, Director Voren was injected with the dose. I was the one to perform the procedure."

Tsuske ignored the banter. His legs felt weak. If it weren't for the director's hand still resting on his shoulder, he did not think he would have the strength to continue to stand. "I don't understand, why?"

"Because he was going to die. Yesterday after the meeting I was concerned for the director and so I paid him a brief visit, to convey to Doctor Axel where he had been as I was sure that he had not been informed of his leave. I was right. Good thing I was there, too. He was going into cardiac arrest as they were preparing him for the prosthetics. I was able to retrieve my latest research vials and gift him a lifesaving dose. A booster to go along with the prosthetics."

"Director, I am so happy that you are alive but why do the rest of COBRA need this? To what purpose does this serve? We have fought and died for this empire." He heard a cough come from somewhere in the room, perhaps even laughter, but he ignored it. Only one person held his attention, and it was the man before him. The father that he never had.

Director Voren sighed and looked away, his arm—and the stability with it—sliding away. "I did not choose this for myself and nor did I choose this for COBRA. It is of necessity. Imperative for COBRA to change as the empire changes."

"That is not enough," Tsuske said, stepping away from him. He looked up at the lord emperor who had witnessed the exchange. Every person in the room had, but Tsuske ignored the rest of them. Finally, finding his voice, he said, "Why, my lord emperor? Why do this to us? Why change us from who we are?" Tsuske had just been figuring out his role. He had just started to piece things together to make sense of everything.

The mood in the air shifted, seemed to grow darker. "You will do as you are told, Tsuske, second in command of COBRA or you will die by the knife."

"Give me a reason, uncle, please!" Tsuske implored his uncle, his knees hitting the ground before them all. "If you change COBRA, we will no longer even be human. We will be infused by makra, the same thing that the daemons desire is what we will become. What will become of our humanity? Our human dignity? We will have nothing to live for. Death would be better." He felt his fist hit the ground before he knew what he was doing. "Do not strip us of our humanity!"

The Lord Emperor's eyes narrowed and General Gustaav looked uncomfortable.

"Death," General Gustaav said. "Is preferable than to become something other than human. I commend you, Tsuske, for acknowledging that. If you prefer, I will offer myself to be the one to have the guillotine brought forward." His words were not spoken in hatred, Tsuske thought he sounded… compassionate. A giggle burst through his mouth, shocking Tsuske. When did he ever laugh?

"Now wait just a bloody second there. No one is dying right now. Most especially not my Second. Tsuske," Director Voren's voice spoke to him now. He felt the director standing immediately behind him, felt the heat of the mechanical arm reaching down for him. "Stand up my boy." Then his voice shifted, and he was no longer talking to him. "My Lord Emperor allow me to talk to him for a moment. He has had a rough few days and very little sleep. I determine that you kept him very busy while I was in the hospital."

"Deal with him, Voren. We will meet up later to talk about specifics. I will allow for one rest day. The day after tomorrow is the day for the process to begin. This meeting is adjourned." The Lord Emperor stood and made to leave, his retinue of guards trailing after him. The meeting was adjourned, and the other echelons made to leave.

Tsuske thought he saw a dejected look from the head scientist but he did not care. His world was going to change whether it was tomorrow or the day after.

A firm hand fell on his shoulder and he did not even have to look up to know that it belonged to Director Voren.

Tsuske turned and his eyes met those of the Chancellor who stood nearby. He had not left.

As Tsuske was guided towards the exit, the last thing he saw of that man was a peculiar smile beneath a broad-rimmed red hat and an off-color silver feather jutting out from the back.

Tsuske felt the hand on his back as he was escorted out of the room by the leader of COBRA and only when they left the room, to the sounding grating sound of stone on stone, past the lit flames, down towards the elevator and into the bright cavernous chamber did he realize the hand on his shoulder was not the real one.

Then he remembered the damn hat and laughed.

24

TSUSKE

THE PATH OF ENDURANCE, A COBRA WAY.

The hour hand struck ten when his eyes sought the battery-operated wall clock and he knew that it was time.

With the winter rains casting the lights of day into perpetual gloom and darkness, it seemed well into the evening rather than being late morning. Tsuske was not looking forward to the speech that he had prepared on such a short notice, with very little sleep in him or the time that a normal person needed to process the news he had been told just a few short hours ago. But he was not a normal person, he was COBRA, and they too were about to change. With a calm breath, he stepped onto the podium.

"Good afternoon, my fellows of COBRA," Tsuske began to the cessation of the murmurs below. The room grew still as all attention directed onto him. None seemed to be aware of his lapse of sanity from the night before, for which he was grateful. They would find out, eventually. COBRA were a tight-knit family of a sort, and secrets thought to be well hidden, would become common knowledge amongst his brethren. "As I am sure you have all heard by now, the edict that the Lord Emperor has issued out for the science department, regarding us. I am here to formerly address such rumors and other matters of necessity. Director Voren made me his second in command. He trusts my judgement, my skill and most importantly my delivering this message to all of you. He could not make this meeting as you all may know by now that he had two prosthetic limbs attached to his body recently after losing both his leg and his arm in the assignment in Noterine.

He is still adjusting to the outfitted limbs. He even sneaked off from the medicinal wing twice last night to convene secrets meetings with the Emperor. This did not happen just once, but twice. The second time was much later in the evening that were actually more into the small hours of this morning, and at that time the Lord Emperor's son found him exiting his father's personal rooms and he had him escorted back to the medical wing and is now under lock down for the rest of his healing process under Doctor Axel's care. I give him less than a day to escape from the confines of his, 'imprisonment.'"

Tsuske let the chuckles die down before he continued. "I even heard that he broke the sensory input of the mechanical arm after trying to wrestle several of the honor guard to prove his health and his demands for an early release." He waved down the roars of laughter and then laughed with them. It was exactly like the Director to be in that scenario.

"As he will not be attending this meeting, know that you will all see him on the morrow. He knows the gist of what is being said at this meeting and he approves. Moving on; the rumor you have heard on the edict the Lord Emperor put forward with the collaboration of the science department is true. They are not lies."

A murmur of displeasure ensued. Tsuske did not bother to usher down the rancor that such an affirmation would create. He allowed them their vexation and wide-eyed horror. They would see the truth, just as he did. They would all agree because how could they not? They were COBRA.

"I see the news startles all and concerns many of you. They were a concern for me too. Do not be alarmed. The story of the COBRA is a story of endurance, the resilient snake that made its way to a new planet after being exposed to the zero atmosphere of space. The creature came, survived and thrived and even mutated to giant beasts that the world did not know could create from such a little snake. A formidable snake. We, too, will not back down. We are resilient, we will endure. We are formidable. We are COBRA and we know that ensuring the safety and future of the empire is our number one task and priority. The empire that took in the little snake that made it from a planet so far away, took in a little snake that the rest of the world abhors. They took that snake and made the snake its ally, and the snake gave its allegiance.

It is our duty to do what needs to be done. To do what we must do to see that we complete the task. We are the only department that operates on such a large scale to perform a great many tasks with such few of us to go around.

From reconnaissance, espionage and black ops mobilization. We are not above abductions and assassinations. From destroying an enemy from behind enemy lines without blowing our undercover operation to the less favorable task to babysitting uncooperative echelons and even their children.

We do it all because it is our duty to see the continuation of the Empire. We do the thing that must be done that is inimical for others to perform. We act on tactical division to eliminating potential threats. The empire relies on us COBRA. We are the best for performing the jobs that are assigned to us because there is no other force like us.

One thing our predecessors did not believe was that we would still carry on us to this day.

Our firearms.

Death is lighter than the kel-tech p-32. Living is heavier than the Desert Eagle. Duty, a Glock 22; for its practical, everyday use. Whichever model you prefer as your daily companions, we will do what is asked of us. Duty of ensuring the welfare and continuity of the empire

For those that do not know, and have not been let on and informed of the situation we are all facing, here is our task;

The Lord Emperor and the science department have passed a new requirement of us. They did not think to inform us ahead of time to allow us discord in the matter. We are given absolutely no say in this matter. The decision has been decided for us. We are snakes and know this duty.

Tomorrow, we will begin the treatment of administrative doses of Makra enhancements. They say this procedure to immediately enhance our already superior tactical skills. We are the empire's guinea pigs for this procedure. Let us not fail in the duty that is set out before us because none will cover our backs if we fail. Rest assured that clinical trials have passed with flying colors, we are only the initial field trials to the study. The dosing is expected to be performed with excellent results. Those afraid of needles should not fear, I hear that the Professor Yoshi Nakamatsu and none other will administrate the doses.

From here on out, all new recruits will have to go through this same process. It will be what qualifies future agents for this honorable position. We will need to cooperate with the science department to ensure that the data they receive from these doses will be collected in the subsequent weeks that follow post dosage. You will be required to write down your symptoms and keep track of your daily health for over a month. Any new symptoms that develop over the course of a year will need to be documented and submitted. They will need as much data on their hands to have better results for their later endeavors, I am sure. We will not hinder them or their research.

Tonight, you will receive a message from our boss, Director Voren. He may be charged to lie upon a bed and rest but have no doubt that he has forgotten any of you or will forget his own duties. That man works in his sleep. After receiving the message, it will show a time of arrival and a location. You and your squad mates will arrive at the time Director Voren mentions in his message. Do not arrive earlier and not be late. You are not to arrive outside the designated time allotted to you or your teammates.

I know this seems like a daunting task and an even further arduous requirement to ask of all of you. I feel the same. There are some good and some bad things we should all expect from this ministration. I will go over them briefly.

The bad. Your eye color may change, and hearing and eyesight will be sensitive up to a week post injection. If that is not bad enough for you, the rare changes of hair color and nail pigmentation could occur with possible permanent changes. Still not pissing yourselves. The more promiscuous lot won't be able to get your dicks wet for a week."

At this, there was a mock outrage ensued along with catcalls and boos. Tsuske suppressed the smile and nodded to the assembly seriously.

"There are some good qualities that make us who we are. These enhancements will not change us, they will only make us even sharper. A honed weapon surpassing the edge of sharpness to something more. Those on hormone suppressants will no longer need to have medication after tonight. As holds true for any of you on other prescription medication. Forego any over-the-counter treatments for colds and allergies. I am being told that after receiving the Makra enhancements, there will be no need for any daily elixirs. This dosing should 'cure' most ailments and inadequacies. If you couldn't last a minute before, now you can last an hour or more—in the practice simulators. A bit of a light at the end of the tunnel, eh?

Furthermore, my team, our boss—though the director will only be there to observe if he can—along with myself and agent Dmytro and agent Nileen, will be the first amongst us to receive the injections first thing tomorrow morning. We choose to be first to ensure your comfort and safety.

We will even hold your hands when it is your turn. That isn't a joke. We are family. Each one of you, our boss, and even myself. We look out for our own. Once a COBRA, always a COBRA. In life and in death. We stick by our own.

If all of this is too hard to bear, remember that we are bearing it together. We live for each other. We do this for each other. For the empire. For all that we love and care about.

And as a good friend of mine will say; sometimes you have to do bad in order to do good."

As he looked back at the darkened figures seated in the auditorium, he couldn't help the thoughts of guilt that ebbed their way into his conscious. Much has changed in the last ten hours. Very little for the better. All these lies, all this manipulation—for the empire. For the better good.

They mustn't find out about the mistakes. Not now, anyway.

The moment he stepped back, the organized cacophony of silent bodies coming to attention echoed in the auditorium. He raised his fist to his chest and saluted the COBRA flag. A red snake on a white background:

> *Take your place, do not weep*
> *Dry your tears, your souls to keep*
> *On your feet, we are born to stand*
> *Weapon at the ready, defend thy land*
> *For we are COBRA*
>
> *Stand tall and strike or lay down and die*
> *We do not fear, when death is nigh*
> *Take your place and we will wait*
> *A moment of truth, a day of fate*
> *For we are COBRA*
>
> *Don't be weak in time of sacrifice*
> *Rise or fall, the time is now*
> *Ready your fangs, prepare to bite*
> *Stand your ground, we are in for the fight*
> *For we are COBRA.*

THE END

EPILOGUE

From high above the auditorium, from a viewing point not used for many years, a father and a son sat and watched the proceedings. Director Voren stood in attention. A tear ran down his face with pride.

At least I still have my eyes...

He watched as Tsuske stepped back. The entire company of COBRA coming to attention, the sound echoed softly in the upper portions of the auditorium. Director Voren raised his fist with his men and women and saluted the snake. A red snake on white background. As they chanted, he too silently mouthed the words.

"Father," the youth asked, interrupting his concentration on the snake's way of conduct. "Why are we so tough on them?"

"We never asked them to do more than what they can do."

"Why is it that we make them change?"

"What's your meaning?" The father did not like that his son and heir would question him.

The boy was determined. Director Voren saw it in the curve of his mouth, the twitch of his nose. "Why do we make them change? I think they are outstanding as they are." He had yet to learn the ramifications of what his father could do. He was brave, only so much as one of youth could be brave with very little life experience. He would learn one day. Director Voren pitied the youth. "I do not think I like the head scientist very much."

Director Voren silently chuckled into his hand. No one liked the man. To be liked was not that man's purpose.

"Like or dislike, that has little to do with the proceedings of running an empire. We do what we must, just as they do what they must."

This answer did little to pacify the youth.

"And if this procedure goes awry? You know how often procedures go wrong in the science department. He pushes for results too fast. Look at Director Voren."

"No, he does not. You have been listening too much to Doctor Axel," The emperor chuckled darkly.

"Sometimes," the boy confessed.

"It isn't something that can be rushed. That is not how science works. One must be patient when in the field, and the tests are often mundane. They are laid out so they can be reconstructed as necessary. Every small step and deviance is documented, and a study is laid out. There are a thousand-foot paths to a single study. I have had that scientist in my employ for a very long time. For now, his usefulness outweighs anything he might be lacking in."

"Like humanity?"

"What purpose does anyone have for that? It is either us or them. It is the way of civilization. The betterment of our lives over others."

The lord heir hesitated before changing the subject. "I know you had a visitor last night. I know that Director Voren had something to say to you."

"Do you now? And what did your spying find out?" The emperor sounded amused.

"I was not spying. We can hardly consider it spying when I see him walking down the hallways from your chamber. I happen to live in the same suite as you, father."

"How do you know he was not on official business? Maybe the old bastard was just working?"

The boy scoffed. "Father, that old bastard is one of your oldest friends. The motives were conspicuous. And besides, what happened the previous evening with his Second? I have never seen that man break down like that before. I suspect his motives were pure."

"What motives?" asked the older man, completely ignoring the last part.

"He went to speak with you after departing the meeting yesterday with his Second. This is what I believe—he reported to you any information he had to report and wanted to know the true purpose of your intentions for COBRA and this science experiment. Am I wrong?"

"If you were not my only heir, I would find your presumptions worthy of my ire. You are getting repetitive in your assertions. Heed caution."

Director Voren sensed a darkness coming from the emperor..

"Am I wrong?" The boy pressed. "That it was not his intentions when he arrived at your private chambers late last night?"

"No," the Lord Emperor said, darkly. The father and son moment were gone. The emperor and heir returning to duty. His words seemed to halt the boy in his thoughts. "You put your nose where it not belongs."

"What happened?"

Without answering right away, the lord emperor reached inside his regalia and pulled out a small canteen. "A menial task. Nothing you need to be bothered with." The older man swirled the purple elixir he held.

The lord heir looked at it and frowned. "It is time for you to treat me like a man. Give me an opportunity to prove myself. It is time to give me my trial of rights."

"Why do you want to concern yourself with this? You're only fifteen. You are not ready for the responsibilities of rule."

"I will be sixteen in just a few months. I will be a man and will begin my trials of manhood. Let me begin early. With this."

"You have just a few more months of adolescents ahead of you. Are you sure you want to begin to take on responsibilities? Once you have been seen and give your rights as an adult, you cannot go back to the simpler times."

"I already do more than those of my age. My honor guard and I go to the practice courts down in the Grotto to train. I don't even attend the balls and festivities of my peers, and when I do, I dress as a man of court."

"Yes," mused the older man. "You have an odd fixation with the lower cities. With what has been happening of late, you need to limit your exploits."

The Lord Heir frowned. "Father, are you even listening to me? Give me this opportunity. I am ready."

"What do you think you are ready for?"

"I want my trial of manhood to begin. Immediately."

The Lord Emperor chuckled softly. "And what exactly are you asking for?"

"I want the responsibility of the COBRA."

"You cannot have it."

"Why ever not? I ask this of you, as the start to my trials of a man." His son was adamant. Director Voren watched from a ways off. He noticed as the COBRA filed out of the auditorium. Neat. Organized. Disciplined. The podium was empty now, except for them—not even the honor guard was nearby.

"It is not something to be given. Director Voren has the responsibility of the COBRA. And need I remind you that he already has a second? Your cousin, Tsuske."

"Cousin?" the boy said, thoughtfully, "I have never seen him called that."

"My youngest brother's son. All traitors. All deserving of what they got."

"Father," the lord heir said, his voice coming out in a whisper. "What did uncle Haku Leucii do?"

"Marrying the Higaziit was his first problem." The Lord Emperor growled low. "Voren trusts the boy. Tsuske. I put my trust in his discretion on my blood nephew. I don't understand why you want to have your trials right now. And why you think using the COBRA, for it will garner your nothing."

"I can do it. Just give me this chance."

The lord emperor's face was a mixture of pensive brooding. "Fine. If that is something you wish to put upon yourself, then see to it. I'll inform Voren. He can give you something to occupy yourself with."

"I will do this, father. You will not regret this. We can shepherd them on the right path."

"They do not need shepherding, something you will find out quickly. You may learn from them, since that is what you choose as your trial. Do not disrupt their daily work or utilize them for your own gain. They are the empires and will see to the running's that we rarely have to worry about. And this is your trial; you will learn from them, you will learn their ways, and you will run and succeed on a mission that I provide them. You have one year to see to this end. After that—well, we shall see."

"Yes, father." Silently, the lord heir rose, "I will see to this right away. I will do this. You learned from General Gustaav so long ago and I will learn from your closest friend, Director Voren!"

After a time, the main stage lights automatically turned off, casting the auditorium into darkness. Only the exit lights to the upper chambers of the auditorium brought light to the shadows. The lord heir stood, bowed and left his father seated in the dark. His entourage of guards would be waiting right outside the door.

Which meant there were only two of them left now in the auditorium. Alone. Only a few overhead lights shun down on the seats. After a time, the old Emperor looked up to see a shadow standing near the railing, a man silhouetted in the light. Director Voren strode towards him. Director Voren was that shadow.

"I see you have come."

The Lord Emperor was sitting in darkness, he was adorned in dark regal fatigues of the imperial line and he was darkness itself. "Are they ready for tomorrow?"

"Yes," Director Voren said.

The Lord Emperor with a wry smile on his face. "Anything I should be worried about?"

"Everything and very little."

"Is that so?" The Lord Emperor mused. "My son has a fancy for your snakes. Whatever did you do to impress the boy?"

Director Voren chuckled, "the question you ought to ask is what have I not done to impress the boy, mate?"

"Indeed?"

"I am glad he has chosen this path on his own. Or did you manipulate him into thinking this was his idea?"

"Manipulate is a big word for an old man like me, Voren. As a father, I like to use the word sway, or perhaps I directed him," the Lord Emperor said. "I don't care how he gets there but as long as he is on the correct path, that is that matters."

"I'll see what I can do for the boy to prepare him for his duties."

"See that you do. I fear that we have little time left."

"You sure this is the route you wish to take?" Director Voren stared at the emperor, sensing something from the man. Was he afraid?

"We all die, eventually. Let's hope my time isn't soon."

"All this to save the world?" Director Voren asked.

"All this to save the world," the emperor agreed.

AFTERWORD

Dear reader,

Thank you for taking the time to read my second book written and published.

It means the world to me, from the bottom of my heart to know that you made it this far, again. It gives me hope that perhaps I am to a terrible writer after all. Thank you for sharing in this moment with me.

A request for my readers, if you happen to have a copy of my book, or even the ebook on your kindle, please share a photo with me on my FB page or twitter. Let me know that you're reading one of my books. Tell me about it. How do you feel? I'd love to hear from you.

And lastly, please leave a review. Reviews help the world know that the author exists. I value your feedback.

I hope you enjoyed this second installment to COBRA files, Spirit of the Ancients.

There will be more coming to you soon.

Mercedez

ABOUT THE AUTHOR

Mercedez Rose grew up in the temperate Pacific Northwest where it's cloudy most of the year with always the chance of rainfall. She met her husband over a discussion of his dental hygiene and she knew he was the one as the floss flew wild. Although she is surrounded by the beauties of humanity, her heart beats in tandem to the flight of the umbrella cockatoo as it flies over the rainforest of Indonesia.

With her love of the comical and sometimes aggressive fluffy marshmallows known as white cockatoos, she has woven a world where chaos and magic aren't the only wonders to explore.

ALSO BY MERCEDEZ ROSE

Books part of the Spirit of The Ancients series:

COBRA Files Book 1, Spirit of The Ancients

www.ingramcontent.com/pod-product-compliance
Lightning Source LLC
Chambersburg PA
CBHW031609240626
47153CB00002B/691

* 9 7 8 1 5 1 3 6 5 7 6 0 8 *